36 ft

30 ft

24 ft

18 ft

12 ft

6 ft

eratops   **Tyrannosaurus rex**   **Velociraptor**

Dinosaurs

Arnaud Plumeri • Story
Bloz • Art
Maëla Cosson • Color

New York

Dinosaurs Graphic Novels Available from PAPERCUTZ™

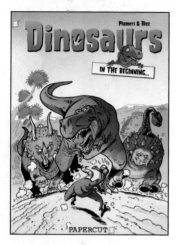

Graphic Novel #1
"In the Beginning…"

Graphic Novel #2
"Bite of the Albertosaurus"

Graphic Novel #3
"Jurassic Smarts"

A big thank you to Ronan Allain, George Blasing, Andy A. Farke, Thomas R. Holtz, Scott D. Sampson, and all paleontologists and dino-fans for their support.
The authors

A huge thank you to the Bamboo family, with special mention to Pierre Tranchand, Herve Richez, and Arnaud Plumeri.
Bloz

For Arthur and Héloïse, my beloved twin dinos.
A world of discovery is opening for you.
Arnaud

DINOSAURS graphic novels are available for $10.99 only in hardcover. Available from booksellers everywhere. You can also order online from papercutz.com. Or call 1-800-886-1223, Monday through Friday, 9 – 5 EST. MC, Visa, and AmEx accepted. To order by mail, please add $4.00 for postage and handling for first book ordered, $1.00 for each additional book and make check payable to NBM Publishing. Send to: Papercutz, 160 Broadway, Suite 700, East Wing, New York, NY 10038.

DINOSAURS graphic novels are also available digitally wherever e-books are sold.

Papercutz.com

Dinosaurs

Les Dinosaures [Dinosaurs] by Arnaud Plumeri & Bloz © 2012 BAMBOO ÉDITION.
www.bamboo.fr
All other editorial material © 2014 by Papercutz.

DINOSAURS #3
"Jurassic Smarts"

Arnaud Plumeri – Writer
Bloz – Artist
Maëla Cosson – Colorist
Nanette McGuinness – Translation
Janice Chiang – Letterer
Max Gartman– Editorial Intern
Beth Scorzato – Production Coordinator
Michael Petranek – Editor
Jim Salicrup
Editor-in-Chief

ISBN: 978-1-59707-732-3

Printed in China
August 2014 by WKT Co. LTD
3/F Phase I Leader Industrial Centre
188 Texaco Road, Tseun Wan, N.T., Hong Kong

Papercutz books may be purchased for business or promotional use. For information on bulk purchases please contact Macmillan Corporate and Premium Sales Department at (800) 221-7945 x5442.

Distributed by Macmillan
First Papercutz Printing

COELOPHYSIS

THIS ANCIENT REPTILE, POSTOSUCHUS, IS ABOUT TO HAVE A MEETING THAT WILL CHANGE ITS LIFE...

WHO'S COME ONTO MY TURF?

WHO ARE YOU, SQUIRT?

I'M A DINOSAUR! WHAT A QUESTION! I'M WARNING YOU: QUIT WHILE YOU'RE AHEAD!

YOU LITTLE PUNK! I'M GOING TO PULVERIZE YOU!

ON THE CONTRARY, I'M A COELOPHYSIS, AND YOU CAN'T BEAT MY SPEED!

GET LOST!

=HUFF= PUFFF=

OKAY, FELLAS! I'VE TIRED HIM OUT!

?

YOU SEE, BIG GUY, WE DINOSAURS ARE BETTER PREPARED FOR THE COMING YEARS!

THIS IS HOW DINOSAURS BEGAN TO DOMINATE THE WORLD... FOR 160 MILLION YEARS.

GROOOH!!!

EEKKK

NYUM

YIKKK

EEK

IT SEEMS AS THOUGH YOU'RE THE ONE WHO'S GOING TO GET LOST!

COELOPHYSIS

MEANING: HOLLOW FORM
PERIOD: LATE TRIASSIC (228 TO 203 MILLION YEARS AGO)
ORDER/ FAMILY: SAURISCHIA/ COELOPHYSIDAE
SIZE: 8 FEET LONG
WEIGHT: 65 POUNDS
DIET: CARNIVORE
FOUND: UNITED STATES

MAMENCHISAURUS

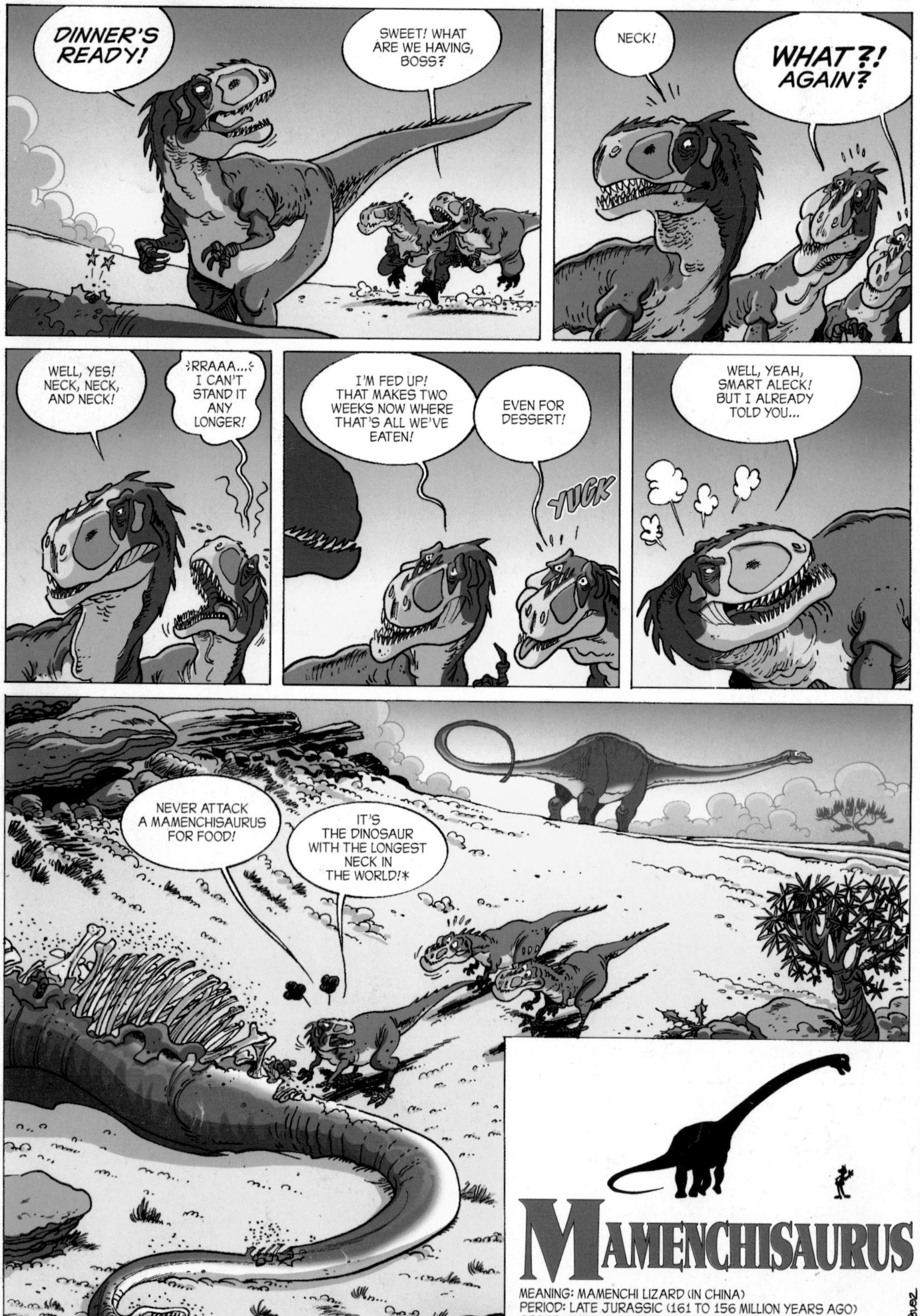
DINNER'S READY!
SWEET! WHAT ARE WE HAVING, BOSS?
NECK!
WHAT?! AGAIN?
WELL, YES! NECK, NECK, AND NECK!
RRAAA... I CAN'T STAND IT ANY LONGER!
I'M FED UP! THAT MAKES TWO WEEKS NOW WHERE THAT'S ALL WE'VE EATEN!
EVEN FOR DESSERT!
YUCK
WELL, YEAH, SMART ALECK! BUT I ALREADY TOLD YOU...
NEVER ATTACK A MAMENCHISAURUS FOR FOOD!
IT'S THE DINOSAUR WITH THE LONGEST NECK IN THE WORLD!*
MAMENCHISAURUS
MEANING: MAMENCHI LIZARD (IN CHINA)
PERIOD: LATE JURASSIC (161 TO 156 MILLION YEARS AGO)
ORDER/ FAMILY: SAURISCHIA/ MAMENCHISAURIDAE
SIZE: 80 FEET LONG
WEIGHT: 45,000 POUNDS
DIET: HERBIVORE
FOUND: CHINA

*45 FEET LONG!

A QUESTION OF WEIGHT

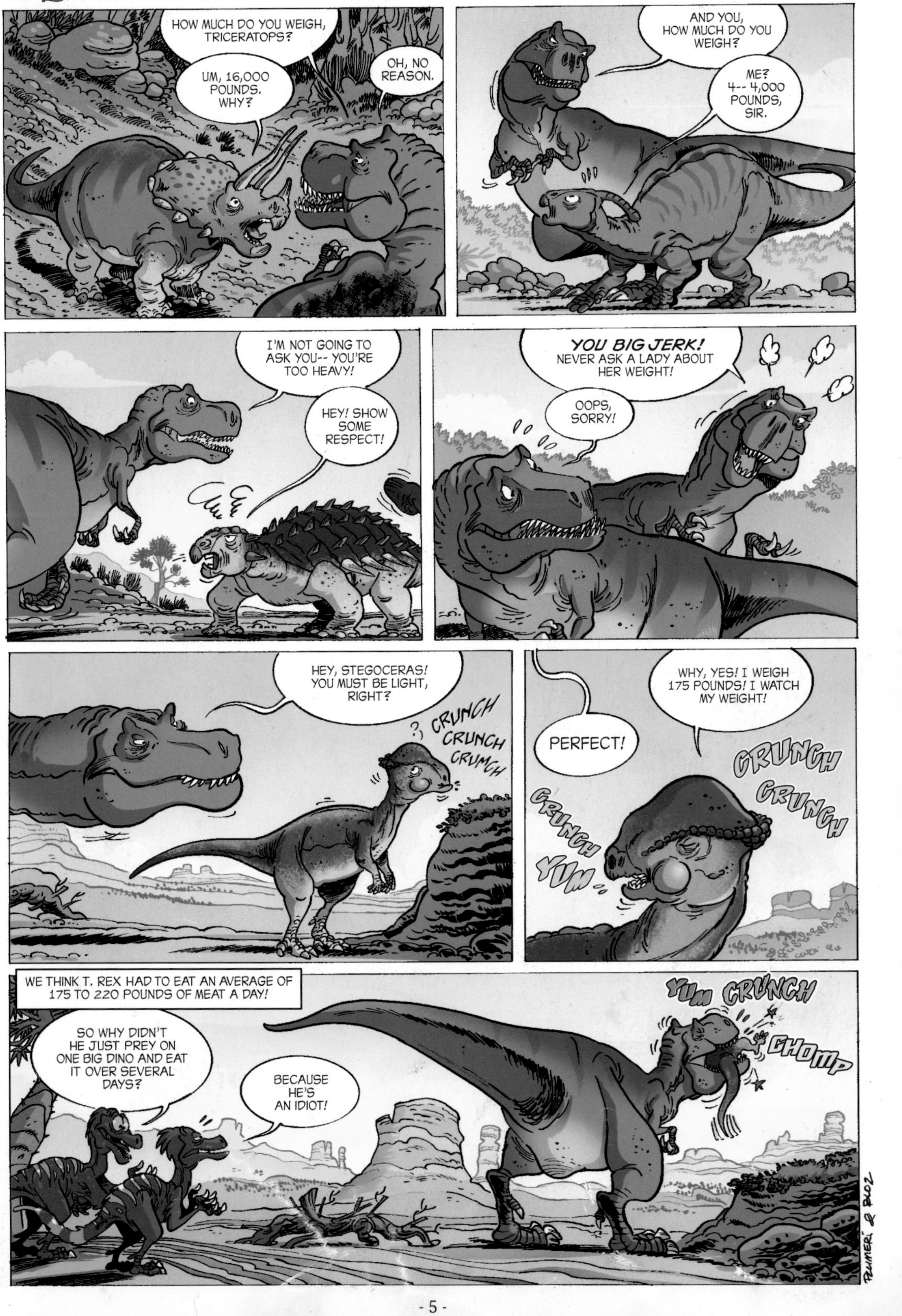
HOW MUCH DO YOU WEIGH, TRICERATOPS?
UM, 16,000 POUNDS. WHY?
OH, NO REASON.
AND YOU, HOW MUCH DO YOU WEIGH?
ME? 4-- 4,000 POUNDS, SIR.
I'M NOT GOING TO ASK YOU-- YOU'RE TOO HEAVY!
HEY! SHOW SOME RESPECT!
YOU BIG JERK! NEVER ASK A LADY ABOUT HER WEIGHT!
OOPS, SORRY!
HEY, STEGOCERAS! YOU MUST BE LIGHT, RIGHT?
CRUNCH CRUNCH CRUNCH
WHY, YES! I WEIGH 175 POUNDS! I WATCH MY WEIGHT!
PERFECT!
CRUNCH CRUNCH CRUNCH YUM
WE THINK T. REX HAD TO EAT AN AVERAGE OF 175 TO 220 POUNDS OF MEAT A DAY!
YUM CRUNCH
CHOMP
SO WHY DIDN'T HE JUST PREY ON ONE BIG DINO AND EAT IT OVER SEVERAL DAYS?
BECAUSE HE'S AN IDIOT!

OVIRAPTOR

MEANING: EGG THIEF
PERIOD: LATE CRETACEOUS (85 TO 70 MILLION YEARS AGO)
ORDER/ FAMILY: SAURISCHIA/ OVIRAPTORIDAE
SIZE: 2.5 FEET LONG
WEIGHT: 65 POUNDS
DIET: OMNIVORE?
FOUND: MONGOLIA

THE LAST FOSSIL I FOUND? THAT WAS QUITE AN ADVENTURE!

MEETING WITH A PALEONTLOLOGIST

I FLEW TO SOUTH AMERICA, BUT I CRASHED IN THE AMAZON RAINFOREST...

I WAS ABLE TO SUBDUE THE WILD BEASTS WITH MY WHIP!

TOMCAT VILLAIN!

ROAR

AND I GOT A STRANGE WELCOME FROM THE LOCAL POPULATION.

Puff!

BUT WHEN I WAS HIDING IN A CAVE, I DISCOVERED A MAGNIFICENT DINOSAUR FOSSIL...

WOW! T. REX IS A RUNT NEXT TO THIS!

THAT'S HOW I FOUND THE #1 MEGA-BEST DINO IN THE WORLD, WHICH I NAMED "BUFFDUDEOSAURUS"!

WHAT? YOU DON'T BELIEVE ME?

OKAY, I WAS EXAGGERATING A LITTLE...

ACTUALLY, THE LAST THING I FOUND WAS A FOSSILIZED PERIWINKLE IN MY GARDEN.

THE SHAME!

MEE A PALE

LIKE INDINO JONES, TAKE A GOOD LOOK AT THE STONES NEAR YOUR HOME: THERE ARE SURE TO BE SOME SMALL FOSSILS MIXED IN!

ROOAR

THE HADROSAURUS ARE IN A PANIC...

THEIR WORST NIGHTMARE HAS ARRIVED: MR. T. REX!

WHAT?! YOU'RE ALL THAT'S LEFT? A KIDS' MEAL?

GO GET ME A NICE FAT GROWNUP AND I'LL SPARE YOU, LITTLE GUY!

RIGHT AWAY, SIR!

BUT SUDDENLY, THE T. REX IS IN A PANIC...

ROOOAR!

BECAUSE HIS WORST NIGHTMARE HAS COME, TOO!

SO?!

MRS. T. REX!

WHAT ARE YOU WAITING FOR?! GET THE KIDS SOMETHING TO EAT!

RIGHT AWAY, HONEYBUNCH!

THE FEMALE T. REX WAS EVEN BIGGER THAN THE MALE!

SOUTH AMERICAN GIANTS

WELCOME TO ARGENTINA, LAND OF THE GIANT DINOSAURS!

HEEEEYYY! HEEYYY!

AMONG THESE IS ARGENTINOSAURUS, THE HEAVIEST DINOSAUR KNOWN.

DON'T BE STUCK UP! GO OUT WITH ME!

STOP BUGGING ME! GET OFF MY BACK!

A SAUROPOD ESTIMATED AT 115 FEET LONG AND 175,000 POUNDS-- THAT'S THE WEIGHT OF 13 ELEPHANTS!

IT'S ALSO THE LAND OF GIGANOTOSAURUS, A GIANT PREDATOR!

YUM YUM!

ROAR

!?

THAT'S HOW ARGENTINA BECAME THE LAND OF SUPER-SIZED MEALS!

WHOMP

YEEEOW!

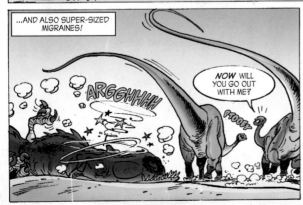

...AND ALSO SUPER-SIZED MIGRAINES!

ARGGHHHH

NOW WILL YOU GO OUT WITH ME?

ROOOF

ARGENTINOSAURUS

MEANING: ARGENTINE LIZARD
PERIOD: LATE CRETACEOUS (97 TO 93 MILLION YEARS AGO)
ORDER/ FAMILY: SAURISCHIA/ TITANOSAURIDAE
SIZE: 115 FEET LONG
WEIGHT: 175,000 POUNDS
DIET: HERBIVORE
FOUND: ARGENTINA

THEY KNEW DINOSAURS

THEY'RE ALL AROUND US, AND YET THEY ALREADY EXISTED AT THE TIME OF THE DINOSAURS...

QUESTIONS FOR A PALEONTOLOGIST

QUESTIONS FOR A PALEONTOLOGIST

CROCODILES, LIZARDS, TORTOISES-- THESE REPTILES LIVED DURING THE SAME TIME AS THE DINOS!

I'D BETTER ENJOY IT WHILE IT LASTS! YUM!

ARTHROPODS, SUCH AS SCORPIONS AND SPIDERS, TOO...

YOU CALL THAT A TAIL, LOSER?!

AS FOR INSECTS, THEY EXISTED LONG *BEFORE* THE DINOS!

HERE'S THE PLAN...

...YOU SUCK THE BLOOD OF THE DINO. THEN WE'LL SELL THE DNA TO SPIELBERG AND BECOME BILLIONAIRES!

YOU COULD ALSO FIND BIRDS (WHICH ARE ACTUALLY LINKED TO DINOSAURS).

¡ARGH!¡

BUGSY!

SNAP

AND DON'T FORGET MAMMALS-- WHICH WERE NO BIGGER THAN THE SIZE OF A DOG.

DO YOU VALUE YOUR LIFE?

PSHHEEE

ON THE OTHER HAND, EVEN IF HE LOOKS LIKE A PACHYCEPHALOSAURUS...

...YOUR GRANDFATHER NEVER MET ANY DINOS!

HA! HA! HA!

STOP LAUGHING ALREADY! I'M NOT AN OLD DINOSAUR!

RUMÉRI & BLOZ

SOMETHING TO SINK YOUR TEETH INTO

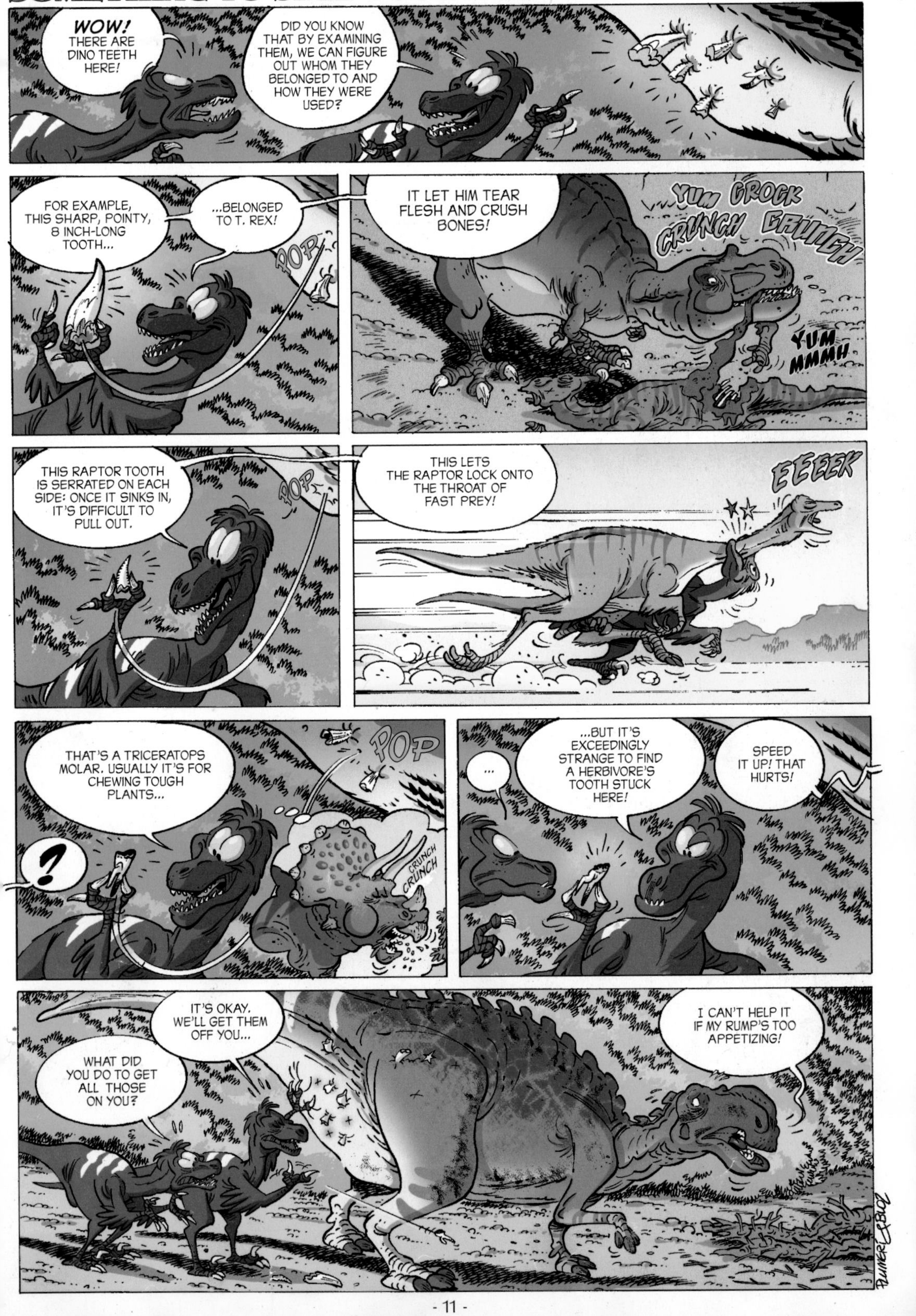
WOW! THERE ARE DINO TEETH HERE!
DID YOU KNOW THAT BY EXAMINING THEM, WE CAN FIGURE OUT WHOM THEY BELONGED TO AND HOW THEY WERE USED?
FOR EXAMPLE, THIS SHARP, POINTY, 8 INCH-LONG TOOTH...
...BELONGED TO T. REX!
POP
IT LET HIM TEAR FLESH AND CRUSH BONES!
YUM CROCK CRUNCH CRUNCH
YUM MMMH
THIS RAPTOR TOOTH IS SERRATED ON EACH SIDE: ONCE IT SINKS IN, IT'S DIFFICULT TO PULL OUT.
POP
THIS LETS THE RAPTOR LOCK ONTO THE THROAT OF FAST PREY!
EEEEK
THAT'S A TRICERATOPS MOLAR. USUALLY IT'S FOR CHEWING TOUGH PLANTS...
POP
?
CRUNCH CRUNCH
...
...BUT IT'S EXCEEDINGLY STRANGE TO FIND A HERBIVORE'S TOOTH STUCK HERE!
SPEED IT UP! THAT HURTS!
IT'S OKAY. WE'LL GET THEM OFF YOU...
WHAT DID YOU DO TO GET ALL THOSE ON YOU?
I CAN'T HELP IT IF MY RUMP'S TOO APPETIZING!

STEGOSAURUS'S PLATES

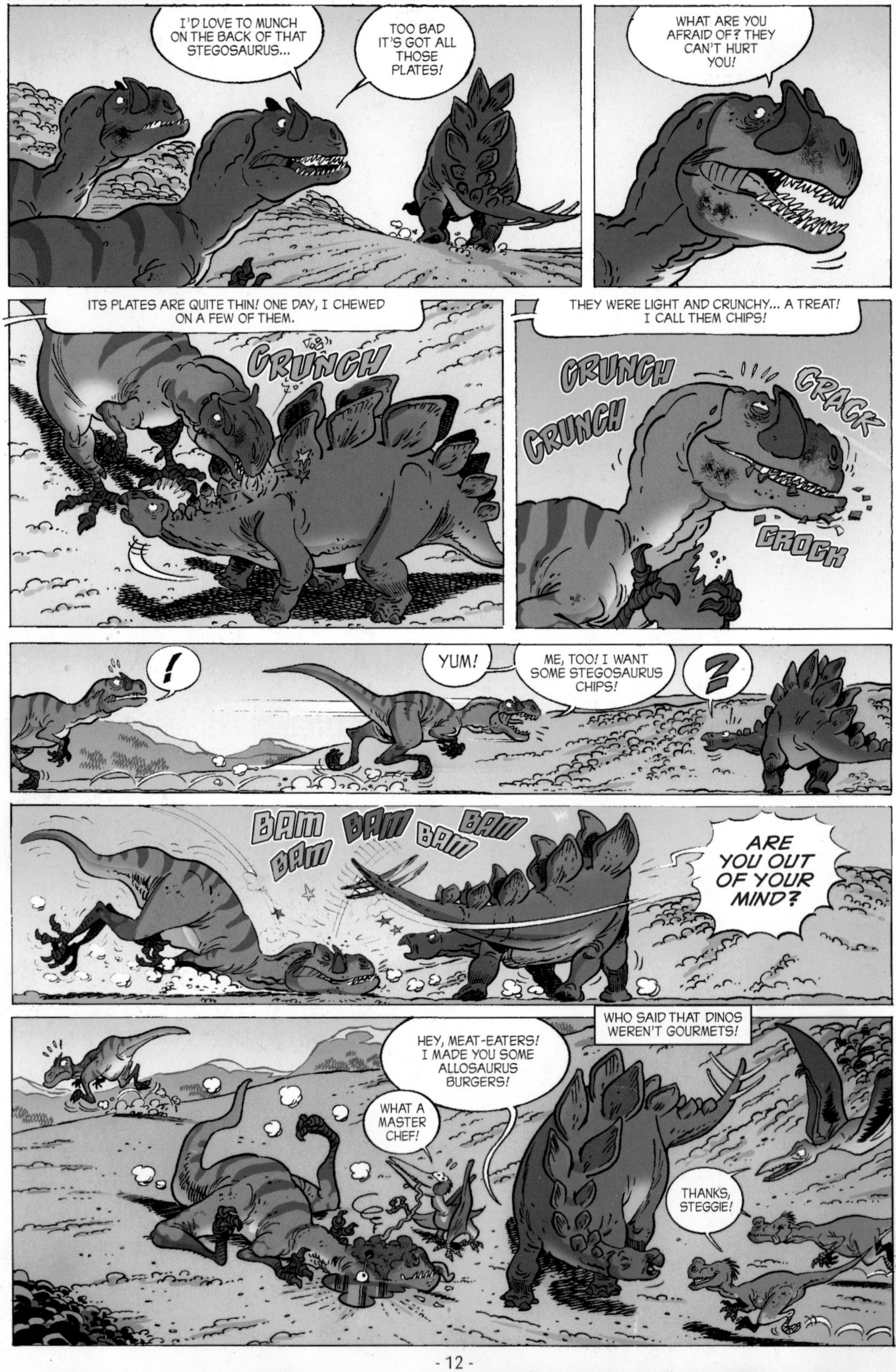
I'D LOVE TO MUNCH ON THE BACK OF THAT STEGOSAURUS...
TOO BAD IT'S GOT ALL THOSE PLATES!
WHAT ARE YOU AFRAID OF? THEY CAN'T HURT YOU!
ITS PLATES ARE QUITE THIN! ONE DAY, I CHEWED ON A FEW OF THEM.
CRUNCH
THEY WERE LIGHT AND CRUNCHY... A TREAT! I CALL THEM CHIPS!
CRUNCH
CRUNCH
CRACK
CROCK
!
YUM!
ME, TOO! I WANT SOME STEGOSAURUS CHIPS!
?
BAM
BAM
BAM
BAM
BAM
ARE YOU OUT OF YOUR MIND?
WHO SAID THAT DINOS WEREN'T GOURMETS!
HEY, MEAT-EATERS! I MADE YOU SOME ALLOSAURUS BURGERS!
WHAT A MASTER CHEF!
THANKS, STEGGIE!
PLUMERI & BLOZ

QUESTION FOR A GLUTTON

STOP, LITTLE ARCHEOPTERYX!

WHA--?

ANSWER MY RIDDLE AND I'LL LET YOU PASS!

GREAT! WE ARCHEOPTERYX LOVE GAMES!

WHO AM I? I'M A DINOSAUR THAT LIVED IN GERMANY AT THE END OF THE JURASSIC...

I'M AN INTRIGUING CREATURE: PEOPLE WONDER WHICH FAMILY I BELONG TO...

I'M A FEATHERED DINOSAUR AND SOME PEOPLE THINK I'M THE ANCESTOR OF BIRDS...

TWEET

BIRDIE?

OTHERS THINK I'M ACTUALLY FROM THE RAPTOR FAMILY...

HE SHOULD HAVE A CLASS!

AND I'M THE FAVORITE FOOD OF CROCODILES. I'M ARCHEO... ARCHEOPTE...

THIS IS SUPER HARD! CAN I HAVE ANOTHER CLUE?

ARCHEOPTERYX

MEANING: ANCIENT WING
PERIOD: LATE JURASSIC (150 TO 145 MILLION YEARS AGO)
ORDER/ FAMILY: SAURISCHIA/ ARCHAEOPTERYGIDAE
SIZE: 2 FEET LONG
WEIGHT: 2 POUNDS
DIET: CARNIVORE
FOUND: GERMANY, PORTUGAL?

WHAT ARE THESE FEMALE CRYOLOPHOSAURS WAITING FOR?

THEIR IDOL: CRYO!

THERE HE IS! IT'S CRYOOOO!

YO! CRYO! CRYO! CRYO! RYO! CR

OH, BABY, BABY, BABY...

HE'S THE DOMINANT MALE...

HE TOUCHED ME! I'LL NEVER WASH AGAIN!

HE'S THE BEST LOOKING, THE STRONGEST... THE FEMALES ARE CRAZY ABOUT HIM!

AND THE YOUNG MALES DREAM OF HAVING A CREST AS NICE AS HIS!

WAAHHH

LOOK! ANOTHER MALE AS GOOD-LOOKING AS CRYO!

YOU WOULDN'T CATCH MAMMALS CARRYING ON LIKE THIS!

SNIFF!

CRYOLO! CRYOLO! CRYOLO!

I SHOULD HOPE NOT!

ESPECIALLY NOT HUMANS!

CRYOLOPHOSAURUS

MEANING: COLD CREST LIZARD
PERIOD: EARLY JURASSIC (189 TO 183 MILLION YEARS AGO)
ORDER/ FAMILY: SAURISCHIA/ DILOPHOSAURIDAE
SIZE: 20 FEET LONG
WEIGHT: 1,100 POUNDS
DIET: CARNIVORE
FOUND: ANTARCTICA

THE FATE OF THE IGUANODON

COME CLOSER AND I'LL USE MY POWERS TO TELL YOU YOUR FORTUNE!

COOL! TELL ME IF I'M GOING TO BE FAMOUS!

I SEE... THAT A GRAND DESTINY AWAITS YOU!

IN 1822, STRANGE MAMMALS CALLED "HUMANS" WILL FIND YOUR TEETH!

MY TEETH?

YOU WILL BECOME A REAL STAR IN A PLACE CALLED "ENGLAND."

I FOUND THE TEETH OF A GIANT IGUANA... HENCE THE NAME "IGUANODON."

THEY'LL BELIEVE YOU HAVE A HORN BECAUSE THEY'LL STICK YOUR THUMB ON YOUR NOSE, THE DUMMIES!

RIGHT, IN FACT, IT WAS A TYPE OF A LARGE RHINOCEROS!

THEY'LL EVEN ASSEMBLE A MEAL INSIDE A GIANT IGUANODON THAT WON'T LOOK LIKE YOU AT ALL!

WAITER! A GLASS OF IGUANODON PERIGNON!

BUT THEY'LL WIND UP GETTING TO KNOW YOU BETTER AFTER FINDING LOTS OF YOUR COUSINS IN BELGIUM.

TOO COOL!

BUT THEN ONE DAY, THESE FUNNY MAMMALS WILL PREFER ANOTHER CREATURE, NAMED "T. REX!"

TEE WRECKS?

?

STOP SCARING ALL THE DINOS WITH YOUR NONSENSE!

BUT I'M JUST TELLING THEM THE TRUTH!

WAAHH! I WON'T BE THE FAVORITE!

PLUMERI & BOZ

SINORNITHOSAURUS

IN OUR TIME, THE KOMODO DRAGON IS AN AWESOME HUNTER...

SNAP

EEEEE

...DUE TO ITS POISONOUS BITE!

NYARK, NYARK!
IT'S NOT WORTH
RUNNING AWAY.
MY VENOM WILL BUMP
YOU OFF!

LET'S GO BACK 125 MILLION YEARS EARLIER TO LOOK AT THE SINORNITHOSAURUS...

A CHINESE DINOSAUR WITH A VENOMOUS MUZZLE...

SURPRISE,
FURRY
DUDES!

EEK EEK

SPLAT

AT LEAST, THAT'S WHAT SOME PALEONTOLOGISTS CLAIM...

LOOK! YOU CAN
CLEARLY SEE SITES
FOR VENOM POUCHES
HERE!

NO WAY! THAT'S
NONSENSE!

VENOMOUS!
I REALLY DON'T
WANT TO
KNOW...

BUT ITS TOTALLY
ROTTEN BREATH WAS
NO GREAT SHAKES,
EITHER! GHASTLY!

GET UP!

?

SINORNITHOSAURUS

MEANING: CHINESE LIZARD-BIRD
PERIOD: EARLY CRETACEOUS (125 TO 110 MILLION YEARS AGO)
ORDER/ FAMILY: SAURISCHIA/ DROMAEOSAURIDAE
SIZE: 3 FEET LONG
WEIGHT: 9 POUNDS
DIET: CARNIVORE
FOUND: CHINA

JURASSIC DANCE

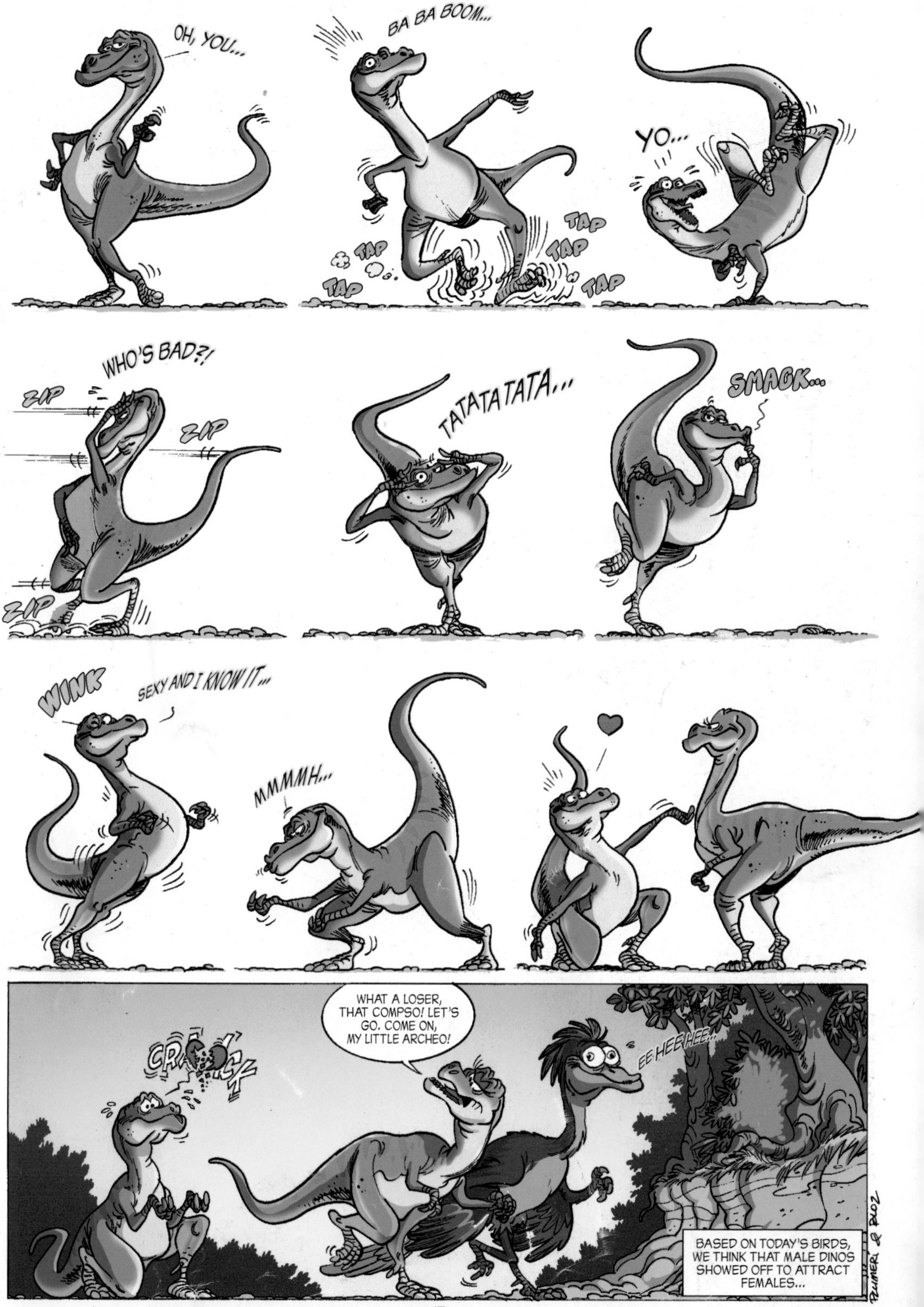
OH, YOU...
BA BA BOOM...
TAP TAP TAP TAP TAP TAP
YO...
WHO'S BAD?!
ZIP ZIP ZIP
TATATATATA...
SMACK...
WINK
SEXY AND I KNOW IT...
MMMMH...
WHAT A LOSER, THAT COMPSO! LET'S GO. COME ON, MY LITTLE ARCHEO!
CRACK
EE HEE HEE...
BASED ON TODAY'S BIRDS, WE THINK THAT MALE DINOS SHOWED OFF TO ATTRACT FEMALES...
PLUMERI & BLOZ

PTEROSAURS

225 MILLION YEARS AGO, REPTILES MADE A BIG DECISION...

RWEEE

AND THAT WAS TO FLY AWAY, THANKS TO THEIR WINGS MADE OF SKIN MEMBRANES.

LATER, LOSER!

THESE FLYING REPTILES, PTEROSAURS, WERE SMALL AT FIRST, WITH BIG HEADS AND LONG TAILS.

IT'S VERY PRACTICAL FOR CATCHING FISH!

THEN, THEIR NECKS GOT LONGER AND THEY SETTLED ACROSS THE PLANET.

IF THEY COULD AVOID SETTLING ACROSS ME, I'D SETTLE FOR THAT.

DURING THE CRETACEOUS, THEY BECAME VERY LARGE, LIKE THE PTERANODON (20 FOOT WINGSPAN)...

AAAAHH

...EVEN IMMENSE, LIKE THE HATZEGOPTERYX, WHICH, WHEN IT WAS ON THE GROUND, WAS THE SIZE OF A GIRAFFE.

WHAT? WHAT ARE YOU STARING AT?

SO UNTIL THEY DISAPPEARED 65 MILLION YEARS AGO, PTEROSAURS WERE THE KINGS OF THE AIR!

NOTHING CAN STOP ME NOW!

BAM

I'M FED UP WITH THIS! THAT'S THE THIRD TIME I'VE GOTTEN NAILED!

OUCH

I TOLD YOU YOUR HEAD'S TOO BIG!

WELL... MOST OF THE TIME!

PLUMERI & BLOZ

T. REX'S ARMS

WE KNOW THAT T. REX HAD HOPELESSLY TINY ARMS...

‡SIGH‡...

AS A RESULT, IT COULDN'T CATCH ANYTHING WITH THEM...

HOW'S IT GOING, BIG STINKY?

COME HERE AND SAY THAT AGAIN, YOU DIRTY LITTLE @✱☆✱!

IT COULDN'T SCRATCH ITSELF EITHER...

RAAAA...

THAT ITCHES TOO MUCH!

NYEEEE

HA!

SORRY, I DIDN'T MEAN TO MAKE FUN OF YOU.

COME ON, NO HARD FEELINGS. SHALL WE SHAKE HANDS?

AH, WELL, I GUESS NOT! NOT WITH ARMS LIKE THAT!

HA! HA! HA!

FOR YOU, I'LL MAKE AN EFFORT. COME SHAKE MY CLAW...

?

OKAY!

SHAKE ALL THREE OF MINE!

BUT EVEN WITH ITS TINY ARMS, T. REX COULD STILL LIFT 440 POUNDS!

EEEEK!

MY ARMS MAY BE TINY, BUT THEY'RE STRONG!

WHAT DO YOU DO WHEN YOU LIVE IN A SMALL TERRITORY WHERE FOOD IS SCARCE?

SUCH MISERY!

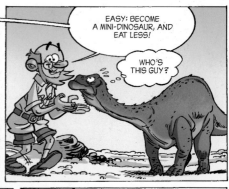

EASY: BECOME A MINI-DINOSAUR, AND EAT LESS!

WHO'S THIS GUY?

THAT'S WHAT HAPPENED ON THE SMALL ISLAND OF HATEG, LOCATED TODAY IN ROMANIA.

ALL THE HERBIVORES WERE MINIATURES. BUT WHAT ABOUT THE CARNIVOROUS DINOS?

RWAAAA!

WELL, THEY WERE ALL SMALL, TOO...

GO ON, LOSER, CLEAR OUT!

÷GRUMBBLLL...÷

NO MATTER. I'LL JUST GET MY REVENGE ON THESE LITTLE PTEROSAURS.

THIS DINOSAUR MINIATURIZATION HAS A NAME: INSULAR DWARFISM...

JUST ONE SMALL PROBLEM: DWARFISM DIDN'T AFFECT THE HUGE HATZEGOPTERYX THAT FLEW FROM ISLAND TO ISLAND...

A SMALL PROBLEM? I'D CALL THAT AN ENORMOUS PROBLEM!

HE ATTRACTED A YUTYRANNUS, THE LARGEST KNOWN FEATHERED DINOSAUR!*

YUTYRANNUS

MEANING: FEATHERED TYRANT
PERIOD: EARLY CRETACEOUS (125 MILLION YEARS AGO)
ORDER/ FAMILY: SAURISCHIA/ TYRANNOSAUROIDAE
SIZE: 30 FEET LONG
WEIGHT: 3,300 POUNDS
DIET: CARNIVORE
FOUND: CHINA

*PLUS IT'S A COUSIN OF T. REX!

- 21 -

DID DINOSAURS GET SICK?

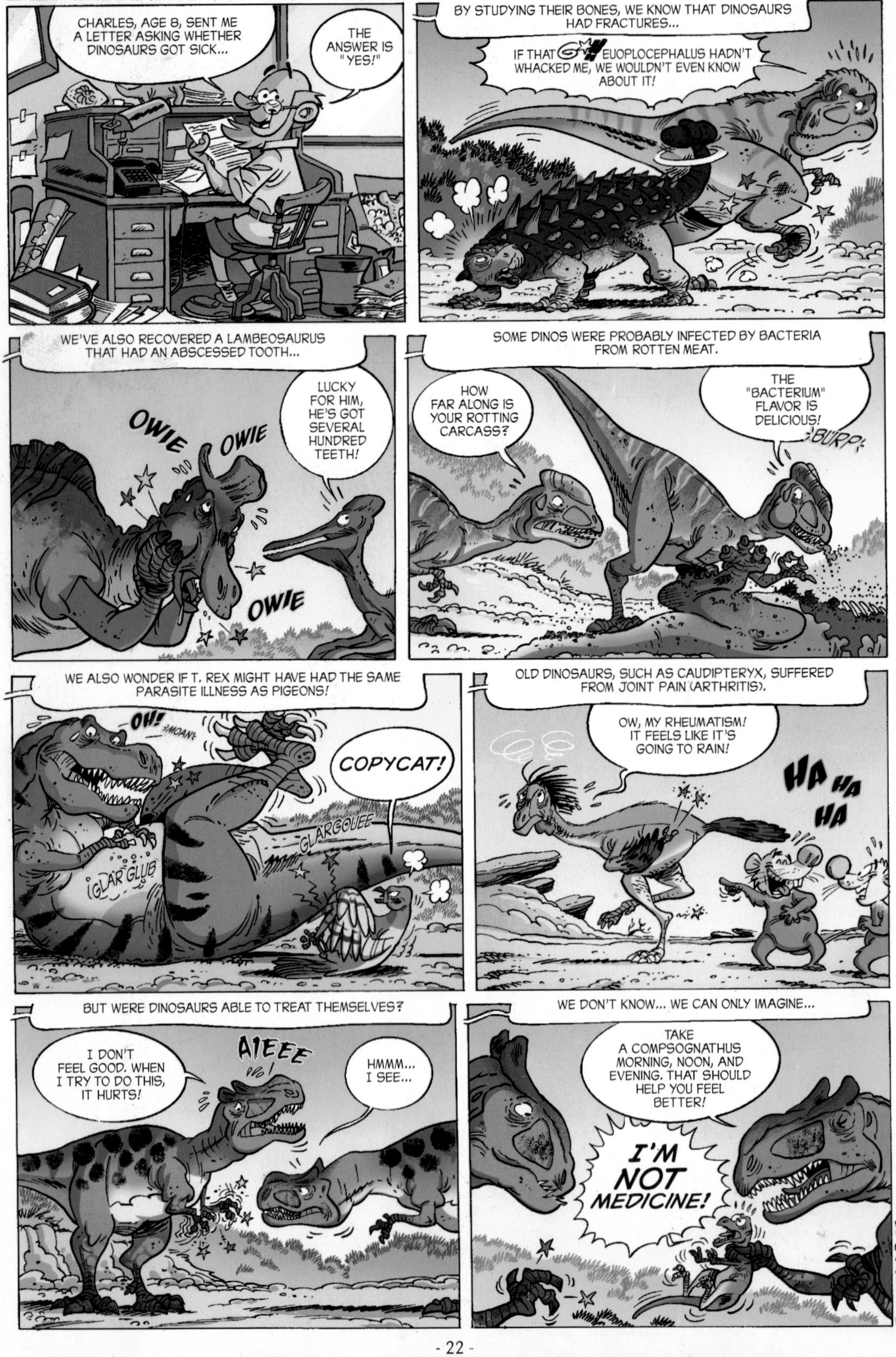

CHARLES, AGE 8, SENT ME A LETTER ASKING WHETHER DINOSAURS GOT SICK...
THE ANSWER IS "YES!"
BY STUDYING THEIR BONES, WE KNOW THAT DINOSAURS HAD FRACTURES...
IF THAT EUOPLOCEPHALUS HADN'T WHACKED ME, WE WOULDN'T EVEN KNOW ABOUT IT!
WE'VE ALSO RECOVERED A LAMBEOSAURUS THAT HAD AN ABSCESSED TOOTH...
OWIE
OWIE
OWIE
LUCKY FOR HIM, HE'S GOT SEVERAL HUNDRED TEETH!
SOME DINOS WERE PROBABLY INFECTED BY BACTERIA FROM ROTTEN MEAT.
HOW FAR ALONG IS YOUR ROTTING CARCASS?
THE "BACTERIUM" FLAVOR IS DELICIOUS!
BURP
WE ALSO WONDER IF T. REX MIGHT HAVE HAD THE SAME PARASITE ILLNESS AS PIGEONS!
OH!
MOAN
COPYCAT!
GLARGOUEE
GLAR GLUB
OLD DINOSAURS, SUCH AS CAUDIPTERYX, SUFFERED FROM JOINT PAIN (ARTHRITIS).
OW, MY RHEUMATISM! IT FEELS LIKE IT'S GOING TO RAIN!
HA HA HA
BUT WERE DINOSAURS ABLE TO TREAT THEMSELVES?
I DON'T FEEL GOOD. WHEN I TRY TO DO THIS, IT HURTS!
AIEEE
HMMM... I SEE...
WE DON'T KNOW... WE CAN ONLY IMAGINE...
TAKE A COMPSOGNATHUS MORNING, NOON, AND EVENING. THAT SHOULD HELP YOU FEEL BETTER!
I'M NOT MEDICINE!
PLUMERI & BLOZ

DILONG

Here's one of the first tyrannosaurs: the Dilong.

Dilong: that means "Emperor Dragon"... so venerate me!

Don't be fooled by its coat: it's not a softie!

ROOOAR!

Because its teeth are perfect for tearing flesh!

Yum yum mmm

And it's a predator that's on the lookout for anything that moves.

Sniff *Sniff*

I smell a big pile of meat!

Sure of its strength, nothing scares it!

Get in my belly!

?

Unfortunately, it's also a tiny dino, much less feared than its cousin T. Rex!

Get out of here, squirt!

No, really.

AIEE AIEE

BONK

DILONG

MEANING: EMPEROR DRAGON
PERIOD: EARLY CRETACEOUS (128 TO 125 MILLION YEARS AGO)
ORDER/ FAMILY: SAURISCHIA/ TYRANNOSAUROIDAE
SIZE: 5 FEET LONG
WEIGHT: 55 POUNDS
DIET: CARNIVORE
FOUND: CHINA

TERROR OF THE JURASSIC

STRONGER THAN THE PTEROSAURS...

STRONGER THAN THE SPINY DINOSAURS...

STRONGER THAN THE BIG PREDATORS...

...AND STRONGER THAN THE GIANT SAUROPOD: IT'S THE TERROR OF THE JURASSIC...

TIP TAP

IT'S PSEUDOPULEX, A GIGANTIC FLEA: WITH ITS HUGE HORN-LIKE SYRINGE, IT TORMENTED ALL DINOSAURS, WITHOUT EXCEPTION!

NICE, FLE-- FLEA, OKAY?

OUCH OUCH

NYUCK NYUCK

SCRATCH SCRATCH SCRATCH

SCRATCH SCRATCH

SCRATCH SCRATCH SCRATCH

AWOOGA AWOOGA

LOOK, UNCLE THAT GUY'S SHOWING OFF IN HIS BIG FANCY CAR.

HEE! HEE! BUT THAT'S NOTHING NEW, ANAIS!...

YOU CAN IMAGINE THAT MALE DINOS ALSO TRIED TO GET THE FEMALES TO NOTICE THEM, IN ORDER TO ATTRACT THEM!

IN THE CASE OF THE PARASAUROLOPHUS, FOR EXAMPLE, THE MALES' CRESTS WERE BIGGER THAN THOSE OF THE FEMALES.

MY IDEAL MAN? BIG, GREEN, AND WITH A CREST THAT IS AT LEAST 6 FEET IN SIZE!

AMONG THE "HORNED HEADS," THE SIZE OF THEIR FRILLS PROBABLY ALLOWED THEM TO STAND OUT.

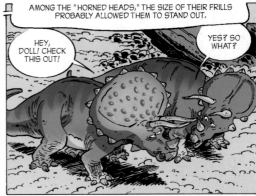

HEY, DOLL! CHECK THIS OUT!

YES? SO WHAT?

WE EVEN WONDER IF THEY MIGHT HAVE USED PRETTY COLORED PATTERNS!

IT DOESN'T GET ANY MORE OBVIOUS OR CLEARER THAN THIS, RIGHT?

GREAT... A ROMANTIC!

AMONG THE "REINFORCED SKULL DINOS," THE PACHYCEPHALOSAURUS MALES WOULD HAVE HAD A RAISED SKULL.

DON'T FOLLOW HIM! IT'S A TRICK! HE'LL LEAVE YOU LIKE HE LEFT ME...

...WITH A QUICK TAP OF HIS HEAD!

?

WE CALL THESE PHYSICAL DIFFERENCES BETWEEN MALES AND FEMALES SEXUAL DIMORPHISM!

ARE YOU LISTENING TO ME?

DON'T LET YOURSELF BE TRICKED BY THIS GUY, LADIES!

THIS IS AN OLD DINOSAUR SEX TRAP!

VROO

PALMERI & BAZ

STOOD
UPRIGHT

BIG HEAD

GROOO...

BIG STUPID
DIPLODOCUS

TAIL THAT
DRAGGED ALONG
THE GROUND...

IN 1930,
WE THOUGHT
DINOSAURS WERE
LIKE THIS...

TODAY,
WE THINK
THEY'RE MORE
LIKE THIS...

WELL-PROPORTIONED
HEAD

ROAR!

SNEAKY LITTLE
BEAST (WHOSE
LIFE IS ALWAYS
THREATENED)

EEEK

TAIL
PARALLEL
TO THE GROUND
TO STAY
BALANCED

SCIENTIFIC PROGRESS
KEEPS LETTING US HAVE
A MORE ACCURATE VIEW
OF OUR BELOVED
DINOS!

FOR EXAMPLE,
WE RECENTLY FOUND
A COUSIN OF T. REX
COVERED WITH FEATHERS,
THE YUTYRANNUS...

TWEET
TWEET?

IF THAT IS SO, IN SEVERAL YEARS, WE'LL
BE DEPICTING OUR GOOD OLD T. REX...

ROAR

WITH
HANDSOME
FEATHERS,
TOO!

HEHHEHHEH HOHOHO
HAHAHA OH HAHAHEEHEE
HOHO HOHO

YOU DIDN'T
HAVE TO MAKE
MY FEATHERS
PINK!

TAP
TAP

LEAELLYNASAURA'S HARD LIFE

YOU MIGHT NEVER HAVE IMAGINED THAT SOME DINOSAURS, LIKE THESE LEAELLYNASAURA, WOULD HAVE KNOWN SNOW!

BRRRBRRRBRRR

THEIR TERRITORY, AUSTRALIA, WAS LOCATED NEAR THE SOUTH POLE.

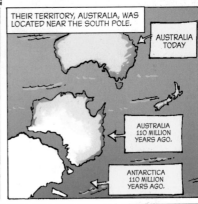

AUSTRALIA TODAY

AUSTRALIA 110 MILLION YEARS AGO.

ANTARCTICA 110 MILLION YEARS AGO.

SO WHAT DID THEY DO TO HANG ON?

WELL, IN THE BEGINNING, THE SNOW WAS FUN...

SNOWBALL FIGHT!

YAY!

WINTER WAS LONG, PARTICULARLY BECAUSE THESE DINOS DIDN'T HIBERNATE...

BRRRBRRRBRRR

BUT NOT SEEING THE SUN FOR 9 MONTHS A YEAR MAKES IT A REAL PAIN TO FIND SOMETHING TO EAT!

I'M FED UP WITH EATING FROZEN DINNERS!

ON THE OTHER HAND, WHEN THE SUN RETURNED, IT WAS TIME TO CELEBRATE: THERE WAS DAYLIGHT 24/7!

YEAH!

THREE MONTHS A YEAR, OUR DINOS WERE ABLE TO STUFF THEMSELVES CONTINUOUSLY WITH EVERY PLANT THEY SAW...

HUUM... CRUNCH! YUM!

CRUNCH!

HOW LONG UNTIL SUMMER COMES?

9 MONTHS! ¡BOOHOOHOO!¡

HEY, GUYS! WANNA HAVE A SNOWBALL FIGHT?

...UNTIL THE RETURN OF THE INTERMINABLE WINTER. LIFE IN AUSTRALIA WAS NOT EASY DURING THIS TIME PERIOD!

LEAELLYNASAURA

MEANING: LEAELLYN'S LIZARD (DAUGHTER OF THE DISCOVERER)
PERIOD: EARLY CRETACEOUS (118 TO 110 MILLION YEARS AGO)
ORDER/ FAMILY: ORNITHISCHIA/ HYPSILOPHODONTIDAE
SIZE: 3 FEET LONG
WEIGHT: 22 POUNDS
DIET: HERBIVORE
FOUND: AUSTRALIA

GUESS WHO I AM?

SOMEONE WHO IS GOING TO EAT YOU!

IF I WERE YOU, I WOULDN'T ATTACK THIS DINOSAUR!

?

WELL, THIS BIRDIE'S VERY YOUNG... WHY ARE YOU CALLING IT AN OLD DINOSAUR?

IT'S NOT A DINOSAUR BECAUSE IT'S OLD...

BUT BECAUSE BIRDS ARE DINOSAURS!

ROOOAAR

THEY'RE PART OF THE FAMILY NAMED MANIRAPTORS, WHICH ALSO HAD FEATHERS.

VELOCIRAPTOR

BIRDIE

OVIRAPTOR

SOME DINOS BECAME SMALLER AND LIGHTER OVER TIME.

PUFF PUFF PUFF

IN THE BEGINNING, THIS LET THEM GLIDE FROM TREE TO TREE, LIKE THE MICRORAPTOR.

YAHOOO

AND THEN, THEY MANAGED TO MASTER FLIGHT.

LIKE THIS.

FLAP FLAP FLA

!

NOW, DO YOU UNDERSTAND WHO I AM, FLEABAG?

CHUCKLE!

GO FIND ME SOME SEEDS OR I'LL CALL MY UNCLE VELOCIRAPTOR!

R-- RIGHT AWAY, MISTER DINOSAUR!

PECK

PECK

OW

CARCHARODONTOSAURUS

LET'S WATCH THIS YOUNG OURANOSAURUS...

PHOOEY! IT'S HOT!

HE DOESN'T SEEM VERY AWARE OF HIS SURROUNDINGS...

AAAHHHH! FINALLY A LITTLE SHADE.

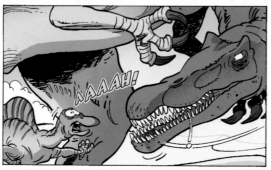

AAAAH!

ROOOAR

IT SHOULD HAVE NOTICED THAT IT WAS HANGING OUT IN THE SPINOSAURUS'S TERRITORY!

WHAT LUCK! THIS WAS ALSO THE TERRITORY OF ANOTHER DINO: CARCHARODONTOSAURUS...

WHAT'S ALL THAT RACKET?

GROO ROAR

A BIGGER THEROPOD THAN T. REX...

?

MOMMY!

...WITH A MOUTH 5 FEET LONG!

EEEE

NOW WE KNOW FOR SURE: THIS OURANOSAURUS HAS NO IDEA WHAT'S GOING ON...

WHAT? WHO TURNED OUT THE LIGHTS?!

HEY! GIVE ME BACK MY MEAL!

CARCHARODONTOSAURUS

MEANING: SHARK-TOOTH LIZARD
PERIOD: EARLY AND LATE CRETACEOUS (112 TO 93 MILLION YEARS AGO)
ORDER/ FAMILY: SAURISCHIA/ CARCHARODONTOSAURIDAE
SIZE: 46 FEET LONG
WEIGHT: 15,000 POUNDS
DIET: CARNIVORE
FOUND: ALGERIA, EGYPT, MOROCCO, NIGER

Microraptor

MEANING: SMALL THIEF
PERIOD: EARLY CRETACEOUS (121 TO 110 MILLION YEARS AGO)
ORDER/ FAMILY: SAURISCHIA/ DROMAEOSAURIDAE
SIZE: 3 FEET LONG
WEIGHT: 2 POUNDS
DIET: CARNIVORE
FOUND: CHINA

ANGEAC DINOSAURS

WE'RE WITH PALEONTOLOGIST RONAN ALLAIN IN ANGEAC, IN WESTERN CENTRAL FRANCE...

HI, MOM!

...AT ONE OF THE LARGEST DINOSAUR DEPOSITS IN EUROPE!

ABSOLUTELY! THIS 8-FOOT FEMUR ISN'T SO SHABBY, IS IT?

IT BELONGED TO A 100-130 FEET LONG SAUROPOD.

!

130 MILLION YEARS AGO THERE WERE ALSO CROCODILES, TURTLES, THEROPODS...

NICE LIZARDS!

AND SOMETHING VERY RARE FOR EUROPE, AN OSTRICH DINOSAUR!

?

TICKLE TICKLE, FIDO!

THE GIANT FEMUR HAD TO BE CAST IN PLASTER AND CUT UP TO BE TRANSPORTED TO THE MUSEUM IN ANGOULÊME... A MOVING MOMENT.

BELOVED FEMUR!

IT'S COMPLETELY BROKEN!

CUT!

POOF

?

YOUCH!

NOTHING SERIOUS. IT'S YOUR FEMUR. IT'S BROKEN.

WE HAD TO PUT IT IN A PLASTER CAST.

YES, I KNOW...

COMPLETELY BROKEN.

SNIFF

THANK YOU TO ALL THE PALEONTOLOGISTS WHO GAVE UP THEIR HEALTH SO WE COULD DREAM!

SHUNOSAURUS

FOR THIS PREDATOR, HUNTING FOR SHUNOSAURUS IS A REAL SPORT!

SNIF SNIF

SNIF

SNIF SNIF

A TREK THROUGH THE FOREST LETS IT SPOT ITS PREY...

JACKPOT!

A REAL OBSTACLE COURSE CHASE ENSUES...

...FOLLOWED BY THE FINAL SPRINT...

ROOOAAR!

...UNTIL THE IMPRESSIVE FIGHT WITH THESE TWO HEAVYWEIGHTS!

BUT THE SHUNOSAURUS IS ALSO A SPORTSMAN...

BAM

NICE SHOT!

THANKS!

EXCEPT ITS FAVORITE SPORT IS GOLF... DUE TO ITS CLUB-SHAPED TAIL!

SHUNOSAURUS

MEANING: SHU LIZARD (CHINESE PROVINCE)
PERIOD: MIDDLE JURASSIC (167 TO 161 MILLION YEARS AGO)
ORDER/ FAMILY: SAURISCHIA/ CETIOSAURIDAE
SIZE: 30 FEET LONG
WEIGHT: 6,600 POUNDS
DIET: HERBIVORE
FOUND: CHINA

ADVANTAGE: MAMMALS

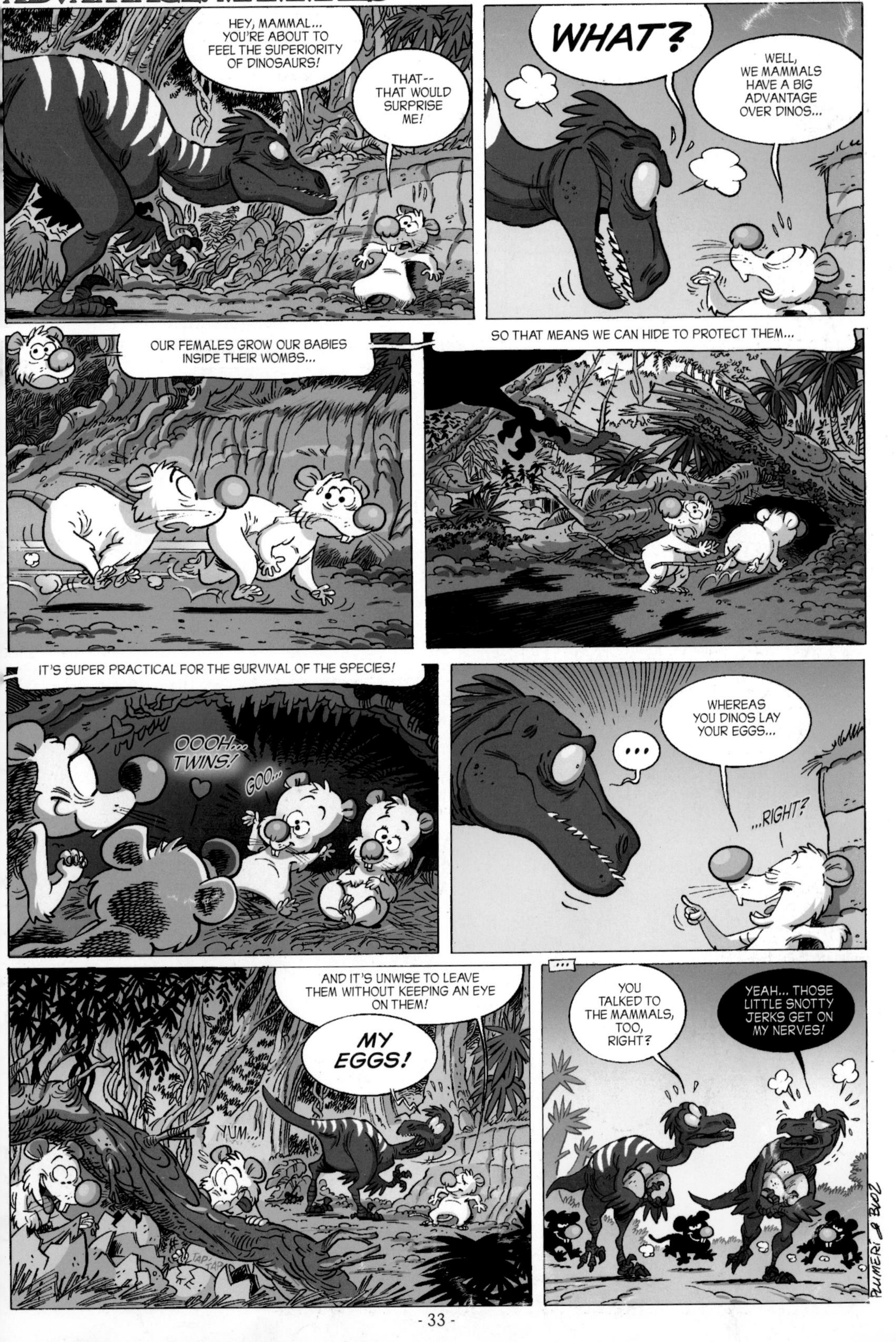
HEY, MAMMAL... YOU'RE ABOUT TO FEEL THE SUPERIORITY OF DINOSAURS!
THAT-- THAT WOULD SURPRISE ME!
WHAT?
WELL, WE MAMMALS HAVE A BIG ADVANTAGE OVER DINOS...
OUR FEMALES GROW OUR BABIES INSIDE THEIR WOMBS...
SO THAT MEANS WE CAN HIDE TO PROTECT THEM...
IT'S SUPER PRACTICAL FOR THE SURVIVAL OF THE SPECIES!
OOOH... TWINS!
GOO...
...
WHEREAS YOU DINOS LAY YOUR EGGS...
...RIGHT?
AND IT'S UNWISE TO LEAVE THEM WITHOUT KEEPING AN EYE ON THEM!
MY EGGS!
YUM...
...
YOU TALKED TO THE MAMMALS, TOO, RIGHT?
YEAH... THOSE LITTLE SNOTTY JERKS GET ON MY NERVES!
PLUMERI & BLOZ

BODYGUARD

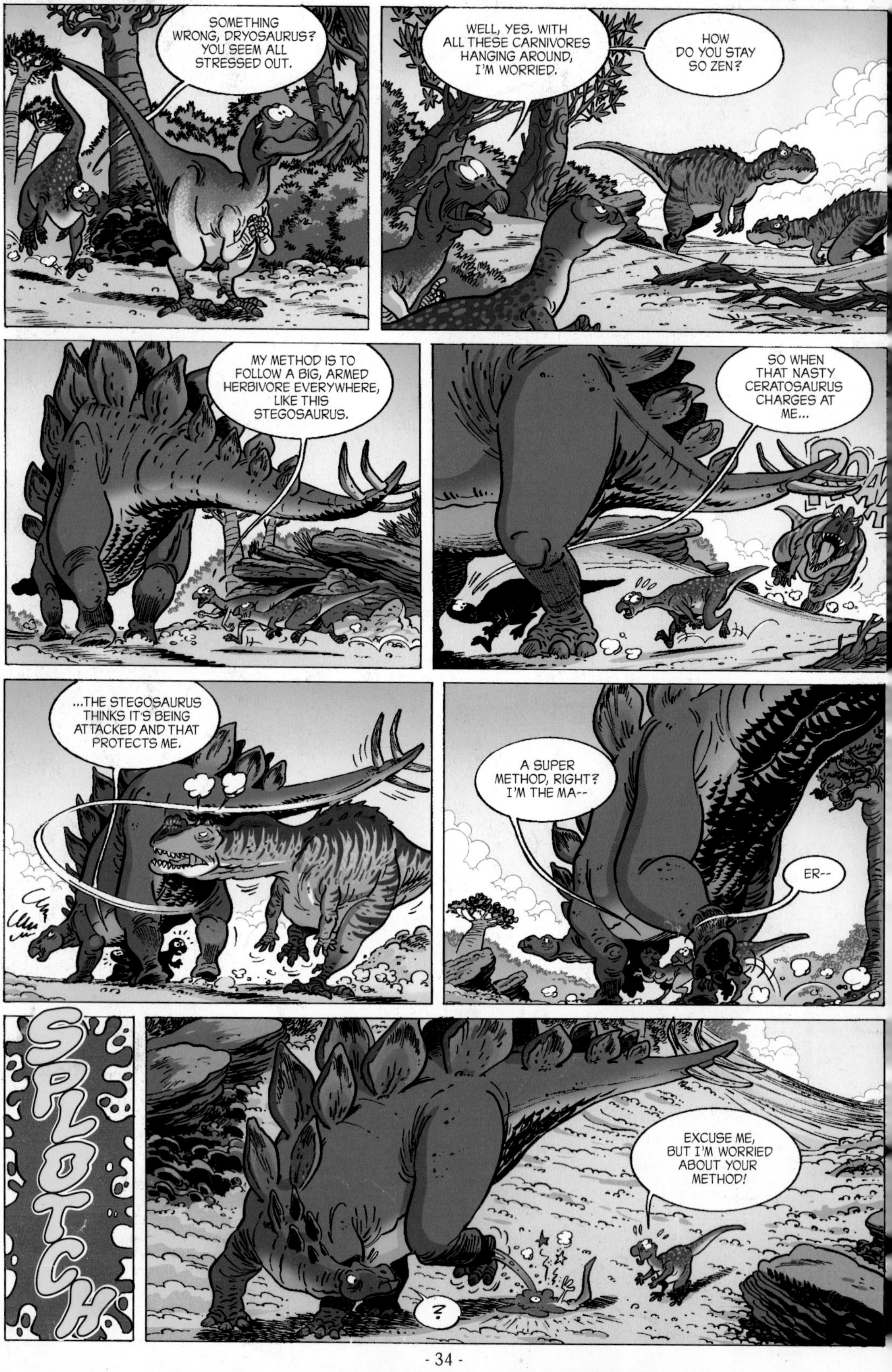
SOMETHING WRONG, DRYOSAURUS? YOU SEEM ALL STRESSED OUT.
WELL, YES. WITH ALL THESE CARNIVORES HANGING AROUND, I'M WORRIED.
HOW DO YOU STAY SO ZEN?
MY METHOD IS TO FOLLOW A BIG, ARMED HERBIVORE EVERYWHERE, LIKE THIS STEGOSAURUS.
SO WHEN THAT NASTY CERATOSAURUS CHARGES AT ME...
...THE STEGOSAURUS THINKS IT'S BEING ATTACKED AND THAT PROTECTS ME.
A SUPER METHOD, RIGHT? I'M THE MA--
ER--
SPLOTCH
?
EXCUSE ME, BUT I'M WORRIED ABOUT YOUR METHOD!

THE MUTTABURRASAURUS WAS HEFTY...
AS BIG AND HEAVY AS AN RV!

THE MUTTABURRASAURUS WAS ABLE TO PRODUCE SOME VERY IMPRESSIVE SOUNDS...

HAAAAWW

THE MUTTABURRASAURUS WAS A MEGA-MOWER. IT COULD COMPLETELY CLEAR EVERYTHING IN ITS PATH.

HEY! YOU OAF!

CHOMP
CHOMP
CHOMP

TO MAKE A LONG STORY SHORT, THE MUTTABURRASAURUS HAD EVERYTHING YOU NEED TO INSPIRE RESPECT.

!

?

BUT WE THINK IT HAD AN ENORMOUS NOSE, WHICH GAVE IT A REALLY FUNNY-LOOKING HEAD.

WAIT A MINUTE! THAT'S HOW MY NOSE ALWAYS LOOKS!

CHECK ITS BIG, STUFFY NOSE!

HEE HEE HEE

ARF ARF ARF

GO BLOW YOUR NOSE, YOU BIG CLOWN!

MUTTABURRASAURUS

MEANING: MUTTABURRA LIZARD (THE SITE WHERE IT WAS FOUND)
PERIOD: EARLY CRETACEOUS (110 MILLION YEARS AGO)
ORDER/ FAMILY: ORNITHISCHIA/ RHABDODONTIDA
SIZE: 23 FEET LONG
WEIGHT: 8,800 POUNDS
DIET: HERBIVORE
FOUND: AUSTRALIA

PLUMERI 8-20-02

SENSATIONAL DISCOVERIES

SOME DISCOVERIES ARE TRULY EXTRAORDINARY. FOR EXAMPLE, WE'VE FOUND...

...THE FOSSIL OF A MARINE REPTILE IN THE ACT OF GIVING BIRTH, PROVING IT WAS DIFFERENT FROM DINOS.

WHAT? YOU DON'T LAY EGGS LIKE DINOS?

NO WAY! I'M NOT A BIG CHICKEN!

...OR EVEN THE EMBRYO OF A DINOSAUR INSIDE ITS EGG...

THIS LITTLE LAZYBONES HAS BEEN SLEEPING FOR OVER 100 MILLION YEARS!

ZZZZ

WE'VE ALSO DISCOVERED A WASP'S NEST AMONG DINO EGGS!

OH, THAT'S WHY MY BUTT STINGS!

BZZZZZZ

AND, MOST FASCINATING OF ALL, IS WHEN WE FOUND SOME MUMMIFIED DINOSAUR FOSSILS...

HERE, LEONARDO: 90% OF THIS HADROSAURUS'S SKIN HAS BEEN PRESERVED!

YLOPHOSAURUS

WHILE WE WERE SCANNING IT FROM EVERY ANGLE, WE LEARNED WHAT FOOD WAS IN ITS STOMACH!

ER, HEY NOW!

STOP SCANNING MY ORGANS!

AND FROM TIME TO TIME, PALEONTOLOGISTS MAKE VERY STRANGE ANNOUNCEMENTS, LIKE THE ONE ABOUT THE BRONTOMERUS...

...A SAUROPOD WITH MUSCLED LEGS THAT DEFENDED ITSELF BY KICKING!

OUCH! A DINO THAT DOES KUNG FU?

WHAT WILL THEY THINK OF NEXT?

AAAIE!

AIEEE!

THESCELOSAURUS

THE THESCELOSAURS AREN'T WELL KNOWN, AND THEY DON'T LIKE IT!

NO FAIR! NO FAIR! WE'RE FED UP! WE WANT TO BE KNOWN!

WHY ARE WE PROTESTING? WELL, DO YOU THINK IT'S NORMAL NEVER TO TALK ABOUT US, EVEN THOUGH OUR NAME MEANS "MARVELOUS LIZARD"?!

AND THERE'S NOTHING MORE THAN A HUGE HEAP OF A TRICERATOPS HERE!

WHY SHOULD HAVING HORNS MAKE YOU FAMOUS?

AND I DON'T SEE WHAT THIS NUMBSKULL OF AN ANKYLOSAURUS HAS THAT WE DON'T!

WE EAT THE SAME FOOD-- AND WE'RE NOT EVEN AS BIG AS HE IS!

HEY!

AND THIS SO-CALLED GENIUS, THE TROODON... CAN'T EVEN HOLD ITS FOOD IN ITS HANDS, LIKE US!

IT'S OBVIOUS YOU'RE WORTH GOING OUT OF THE WAY FOR. I'LL TELL EVERYONE I BUMP INTO--

AH! YOU SEE!

...ESPECIALLY T. REX!

ARE THEY HERE, THOSE AWESOME DINOS THAT ARE SO MARVELOUS TO MUNCH ON?

AAAAAHH

LEAVE US ALONE! WE WANT TO BE ANONYMOUS! WE WANT TO LIVE IN PEACE!

THEY DON'T KNOW WHAT THEY WANT...

THESCELOSAURUS

MEANING: MARVELOUS LIZARD
PERIOD: LATE CRETACEOUS (67 TO 65 MILLION YEARS AGO)
ORDER/ FAMILY: ORNITHISCHIA/ THESCELOSAURIDAE
SIZE: 13 FEET LONG
WEIGHT: 220 POUNDS
DIET: HERBIVORE
FOUND: NORTH AMERICA

PLUMERI 8 BLOZ

THE COMPSO THAT WANTED TO CHANGE THE WORLD

LOOK, KIDS! A BRACHIOSAURUS, THE BIGGEST EATER ON THE PLANET!

OOOOOOH

BUT THERE'S NOTHING TO BE AFRAID OF: IT *ONLY* EATS PLANTS.

YUM... SCRUNCH... CRUNCH...

AND THAT? THAT'S THE ARCHEOPTERYX, OUR FAMOUS FEATHERED COUSIN.

COOO?

OH, COME *ON!* STOP TALKING ABOUT THAT TREE-BOUND MORON!

INSTEAD, ADMIRE YOUR UNCLE COMPSO, WHO'S ABOUT TO CHANGE THE WORLD!

I'M SURE I'LL FIND SOMETHING OR OTHER.

SEE? I CAN CLIMB TREES TO SHOW OFF, TOO!

?

HEY, COME ON...

CRUNCH

SCRUNCH CRUNCH

HELLLLLLP...

GULP!

150 MILLION YEARS LATER...

HERE'S A DISCOVERY THAT WILL REVOLUTIONIZE THE DINOSAUR WORLD!...

PALEONTOLOGY CONFERENCE

...A BRACHIOSAURUS DROPPING WITH COMPSOGNATHUS REMAINS IN IT, PROVING THAT LONG-NECK DINOS ATE MEAT!

RUBBISH!

BOOO!

YUP! I CHANGED THE WORLD!

CERATOSAURUS

MEANING: HORNED LIZARD
PERIOD: LATE JURASSIC (155 TO 150 MILLION YEARS AGO)
ORDER/ FAMILY: SAURISCHIA/ CERATOSAURIDAE
SIZE: 20 FEET LONG
WEIGHT: 2,000 POUNDS
DIET: CARNIVORE
FOUND: UNITED STATES, TANZANIA?

PROTOCERATOPS VS. VELOCIRAPTOR

IN THE GOBI DESERT, TWO NEIGHBORS ARE KNOWN TO HATE EACH OTHER...

I'M SICK OF SEEING THAT VELOCIRAPTOR!

THERE'S THAT JERK PROTOCERATOPS!

YOU AGAIN?

WHAT? YOU WANT TO GO?

GET OFF MY TERRITORY!

YOUR NAME'S NOT WRITTEN ON IT!

BAM

BROLOLOLO

70 MILLION YEARS LATER, WE FOUND THE TWO NEIGHBORS FOSSILIZED IN THE MIDST OF A FIGHT, IMPRISONED IN THE SAND.

SO TODAY, THEY'RE INSEPARABLE ONCE AGAIN: THEIR FOSSILS ARE EXHIBITED IN MUSEUMS ACROSS THE ENTIRE WORLD!

OH, BOY!

IT NEVER ENDS!

PROTOCERATOPS

MEANING: FIRST HORNED FACE
PERIOD: LATE CRETACEOUS (85 TO 70 MILLION YEARS AGO)
ORDER/ FAMILY: ORNITHISCHIA/ PROTOCERATOPSIDAE
SIZE: 6.5 FEET LONG
WEIGHT: 450 POUNDS
DIET: HERBIVORE
FOSSILS: CHINA, MONGOLIA

THE GREAT DISCOVERERS

LET'S PAY HOMAGE TO A FEW BRILLIANT PALEONTOLOGISTS AND THEIR REVOLUTIONARY DISCOVERIES...

GIDEON MANTELL TOLD THE WORLD ABOUT ONE OF THE FIRST DINOSAURS DISCOVERED: THE IGUANODON.

YEEHAA!

SHOCKING!

THE KING OF HUNTERS, *BARNUM BROWN* UNEARTHED THE FIRST T. REX.

ARF! ARF!

GIVE PAPA A PAW!

TH-- THAT'S A GOOD T. REX!

FROM THE DEINONYCHUS, JOHN OSTROM CAME UP WITH THE IDEA THAT DINOSAURS AND BIRDS WERE RELATED TO EACH OTHER.

HERE, BIRDIE, BIRDIE! YOU DON'T LIKE MY SEEDS?

AY, CARAMBA!

HOW AM I GOING TO CARRY THIS THING?

JOSE BONAPARTE SHOWED US THE SOUTH AMERICAN GIANTS, SUCH AS THE ARGENTINOSAURUS.

CURRENTLY *XU XING* AND *MARK NORELL* ARE HAVING A BALL WITH CHINESE FEATHERED DINOS (MICRORAPTOR, ETC.)!

LALALA LALA...

YOU'D THINK THEY WERE IN "SNOW WHITE AND THE SEVEN DWARVES!"

AS FOR OUR DEAR *INDINO JONES*, HE HAS JUST DISCOVERED SOMETHING INCREDIBLE...

MY GOODNESS!

THAT HE HAS A WIFE WHO'S BEEN WAITING AT HOME FOR HIM WHILE HE SPENDS HIS TIME SEARCHING FOR DINOS!

I'M FED UP! I NEVER SEE YOU ANYMORE!

AMARGASAURUS

WITH ITS LONG SPINES, THE AMARGASAURUS WAS A STRANGE LONG-NECKED DINO...

WHAT'S MORE, WE WONDER IF ITS SPINES WEREN'T CONNECTED WITH SKIN TO FORM A SAIL.

THERE'S A THORNY QUESTION!

I PREFER THE SPINES!

AND I LIKE THE SAIL! IT'S UNIQUE!

A SAIL COULD HAVE TURNED OUT TO BE VERY PRACTICAL...

!

ROOOAR

EEEK

DANGER

...FOR INTIMIDATING PREDATORS!

WHAT DO YOU WANT, GHASTLY GUY?

UH... NOTHING, NOTHING!

SAY, YOU WOULDN'T HAVE SEEN SOME LITTLE CRITTERS TO MUNCH ON?

NO!

ALL RIGHT, I'LL SET SAIL THEN!

♪

SNIF SNIF

END OF THE LINE, EVERYONE OFF!

THANK YOU, MISTER!

YOU'RE RIGHT. A SAIL REALLY IS BETTER!

AMARGASAURUS

MEANING: LA AMARGA LIZARD (REGION IN ARGENTINA)
PERIOD: EARLY CRETACEOUS (130 TO 120 MILLION YEARS AGO)
ORDER/ FAMILY: SAURISCHIA/ DICRAEOSAURIDAE
SIZE: 13 FEET LONG
WEIGHT: 22,000 POUNDS
DIET: HERBIVORE
FOUND: ARGENTINA

BLUMERI & BIUZ

INCISIVOSAURUS

INCISIVOSAURUS

MEANING: INCISOR LIZARD
PERIOD: EARLY CRETACEOUS (125 MILLION YEARS AGO)
ORDER/FAMILY: SAURISCHIA/ OVIRAPTOROSAURIA
SIZE: 3 FEET LONG?
WEIGHT: 9 POUNDS?
DIET: HERBIVORE?
FOUND: CHINA

SAUROPELTA

THE SAUROPELTA HAS A KNACK FOR IRRITATING THE DEINONYCHUS...

HEY, A SAUROPELTA!

IT GETS ON MY NERVES! IT PAYS NO ATTENTION TO US!

WE'LL SHOW THAT HOT DOG!

YEAH!

TO START WITH, THEY HAVE TO AVOID ITS POWERFUL TAIL STRIKES...

AND WHEN THE SAUROPELTA LIES FLAT ON THE GROUND, IT'S HARD TO FIND A WEAKNESS...

BECAUSE THIS DINOSAUR IS ARMORED ALL OVER...

SNAP CRACK

OUCH!

TRY ATTACKING ITS NECK!

...AND ITS SPINES ARE WELL POSITIONED TO PREVENT VICIOUS ATTACKS.

I CAN'T!

IN ADDITION, EVEN THE SAUROPELTA'S EYELIDS HAVE A LAYER OF ARMOR!

HEY! THIS BIG RUDE DUDE'S SLEEPING WHILE WE'RE ATTACKING HIM!

HE GETS ON MY NERVES!

ZZZZZ

SAUROPELTA

MEANING: LIZARD SHIELD
PERIOD: EARLY CRETACEOUS (118 TO 110 MILLION YEARS AGO)
ORDER/ FAMILY: ORNITHISCHIA/ NODOSAURIDAE
SIZE: 24 FEET LONG
WEIGHT: 6,600 POUNDS
DIET: HERBIVORE
FOUND: UNITED STATES

WHO'S THE STRONGEST?

ARCHIE! HERE ARE TWO MORE KIDS FOR YOU!

WHAT BRINGS YOU HERE? MORE QUESTIONS ABOUT DINOS?

YUP! WE'VE GOT LOTS OF THEM! TELL US...

ENOUGH ALREADY...

WHICH IS STRONGER, ALLOSAURUS OR CERATOSAURUS?

ALLOSAURUS. IT HAS A MORE POWERFUL BITE.

AND BETWEEN A CARCHARODONTOSAURUS AND A DELTADROMEUS, WHICH WOULD WIN?

THE DELTADROMEUS DOESN'T HAVE A CHANCE IF IT DOESN'T RUN AWAY!

AND BETWEEN A MAPUSAURUS AND A GIGANOTOSAURUS?

⁘OOF!⁘ LET'S SAY... THE GIGANOTOSAURUS IF IT'S NOT CONSTIPATED?

SO, OTHER THAN FIGHTING, IS THERE ANYTHING ELSE THAT INTERESTS YOU?

⁘GRR⁙

PING

CRASH

MY MOTHER'S VASE! ADMIT YOU DID IT ON PURPOSE!

NO, DA-- DARLING...

AND A FIGHT BETWEEN INDINO JONES AND HIS WIFE?

HIS WIFE, NO QUESTION!

TOTALLY!

WHAT WE DON'T KNOW

DINO BONES STEADILY YIELD UP THEIR SECRETS TO US...

GIVEN THE SIZE OF THIS FEMUR, THIS DINO MUST HAVE BEEN 80 FEET LONG!

BUT IT'S VERY RARE TO DISCOVER SOFT TISSUE...

SOFT TISSUE IS YOUR SKIN, YOUR MUSCLES, YOUR ORGANS...

STOP TALKING ABOUT MY ORGANS IN FRONT OF EVERYONE!

AS A MATTER OF FACT, PALEONTOLOGISTS ASK THEMSELVES QUESTIONS. FOR EXAMPLE...

DID THE DIPLODOCUS HAVE A TRUNK LIKE AN ELEPHANT?

CHOMP

THAT COULD HAVE BEEN VERY PRACTICAL!

CHOMP

COULD THE DILOPHOSAURUS FAN OUT A FRILL AROUND ITS NECK?

JURASSIC PARK

SOMETHING ELSE DREAMED UP IN "JURASSIC PARK," MR. SPIELBERG?

AND EVEN COMICBOOK AUTHORS ASK THEMSELVES QUESTIONS.

ZZZ.

HELLO, BLOZZIE? IT'S ARNAUD. I WAS READING SOME STUFF ABOUT BRACHIOSAURUS...

PINK FLOYD

IT SEEMS THAT THERE ARE FIVE POSSIBLE PLACES FOR THEIR NOSTRILS.

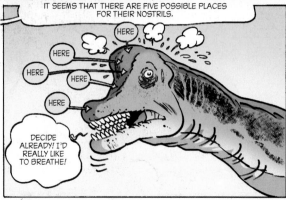

HERE
HERE
HERE
HERE
HERE

DECIDE ALREADY! I'D REALLY LIKE TO BREATHE!

SO THAT MEANS WE'RE GOING TO HAVE TO REDRAW THE FIRST THREE BOOKS!

RHAAAA

HELLO?

HELLO?

RIP!
RIP!
RIP!

I CAN'T WAIT FOR THE ANSWERS TO ALL OUR QUESTIONS!

WATCH OUT FOR PAPERCUTZ ™

Welcome to the T-rex-filled third DINOSAURS graphic novel by Arnaud Plumeri and Bloz from Papercutz, the wannabe paleontologists dedicated to publishing great graphic novels for all ages! I'm Jim Salicrup, the Editor-in-Chief and full-fledged fossil, here to give you a playful peek at some of the other Papercutz graphic novels either in the works, or available to you right now...

Once upon a time, there was a prime-time animated TV series that featured dinosaurs—that show, inspired somewhat by an earlier live action TV series, *The Honeymooners*, was called *The Flintstones*. It featured "a modern Stone Age family" consisting of Fred, Wilma, and Pebbles Flintstone, and their pet Snorkasaurus, Dino. As all you budding paleontologists already know—dinosaurs and humans never were alive at the same time (unless you consider birds dinosaurs, which some paleontologists do). As we all know, dinosaurs first appeared 231.4 million years ago, and hung around for 135 million years. Humans, on the other hand, didn't show up until about 2.3 million years ago, so clearly *The Flintstones* were pure fantasy. Now there's a YouTube sensation called *Annoying Orange* (that was also made into a Cartoon Network series) that also inspired a series of graphic novels published by Papercutz. In ANNOYING ORANGE #6 "My Little Baloney," artist/writer and big-time *Flintstones* fan, Scott Shaw! contributes "Fruitstones, Meet the Fruitstones!" and we'll give you just one guess at what this story happens to lovingly parody! If you thought *The Flintstones* were unbelievable, just wait til we add some talking fruit to the mix! Here's a panel from the first page, still in black and white—we haven't even colored it yet!—of some plastic dinosaurs being played with by Orange and his fruity friends:

ANNOYING ORANGE ™ & © Annoying Orange, Inc. Used under license by 14th Hour Productions, LLC.

Over the years it seems I've edited quite a few comics with dinosaurs in them. Over at Topps Comics, back in the 90s I edited both a CADILLACS AND DINOSAURS series based on the comics by Mark Schultz and a JURASSIC PARK series*, based on the Spielberg movie (based on the Michael Crichton novel). *Jurassic Park*, if by some chance you've never seen it, actually came up with a clever way of mixing humans and dinosaurs—genetically reconstructing them from their DNA, which was preserved in various fossils. It's a scary idea that may possibly even come true one day. But there's a comics series I had absolutely nothing to do with, created by Stuart Fischer– it only lasted two issues, and it was called MANOSAURS. And it went a step further—it created several dinosaur/human hybrids! Originally published in 1993, this series might have been a little ahead of its time, but it'll soon be getting a second chance! Coming soon from Papercutz will be an all-new MANOSAURS series that should be a lot of fun! We'll let you know more as soon as we can on Papercutz.com!

And if you're one of those future-paleontologists who also considers birds to be dinosaurs, then let me tell you about one more dinosaur title from Papercutz: RIO! Based on the animated movies featuring the near extinct blue macaws, Blu and Jewel, and their human guardians former bookstore owner Linda Gunderson and ornithologist Túlio Monteiro. RIO #1 "Snakes Alive!" is available everywhere now.

But if you're a true DINOSAURS traditionalist, then you'll want more of the DINOSAURS graphic novels by Arnaud Plumeri and Bloz, that feature lots of dinosaur facts mixed in with a little fun. And while we're all waiting for the fourth graphic novel—we've got a big surprise for you! We'll be collecting DINOSAURS #1 through #3 in one big volume that will be in 3-D! It'll be all the comics you love in a way you've never seen 'em before! All I can say is: don't miss it! But for something completely different, check out the preview of LEGO® LEGENDS OF CHIMA #1 "High Risk" on the following pages. It's awesome!

Thanks,

Jim

Bonus: Special excerpt from Salicrupedia...
Salicrupsaurus (Page 47)
Meaning: Big-Headed Editor
Period: Bronze Age to Modern Age (57 Years Ago)
Order/ Family: Geekasaurs/ Salicrupidae
Size: 6'2"
Weight: 250 lbs.?
Diet: Omnivore
Found: North America (If found, return to Papercutz)

STAY IN TOUCH!

EMAIL: salicrup@papercutz.com
WEB: papercutz.com
TWITTER: @papercutzgn
FACEBOOK: PAPERCUTZGRAPHICNOVELS
MAIL: Papercutz, 160 Broadway,
     Suite 700, East Wing, New York, NY 10038

*IDW, the comics publisher, has reprinted the Jurassic Park comics adaptation by Walter Simonson (even his signature looks like a dinosaur!), Gil Kane, and George Perez, that I edited, as CLASSIC JURASSIC PARK Vol. 1, and it's still available from IDW.

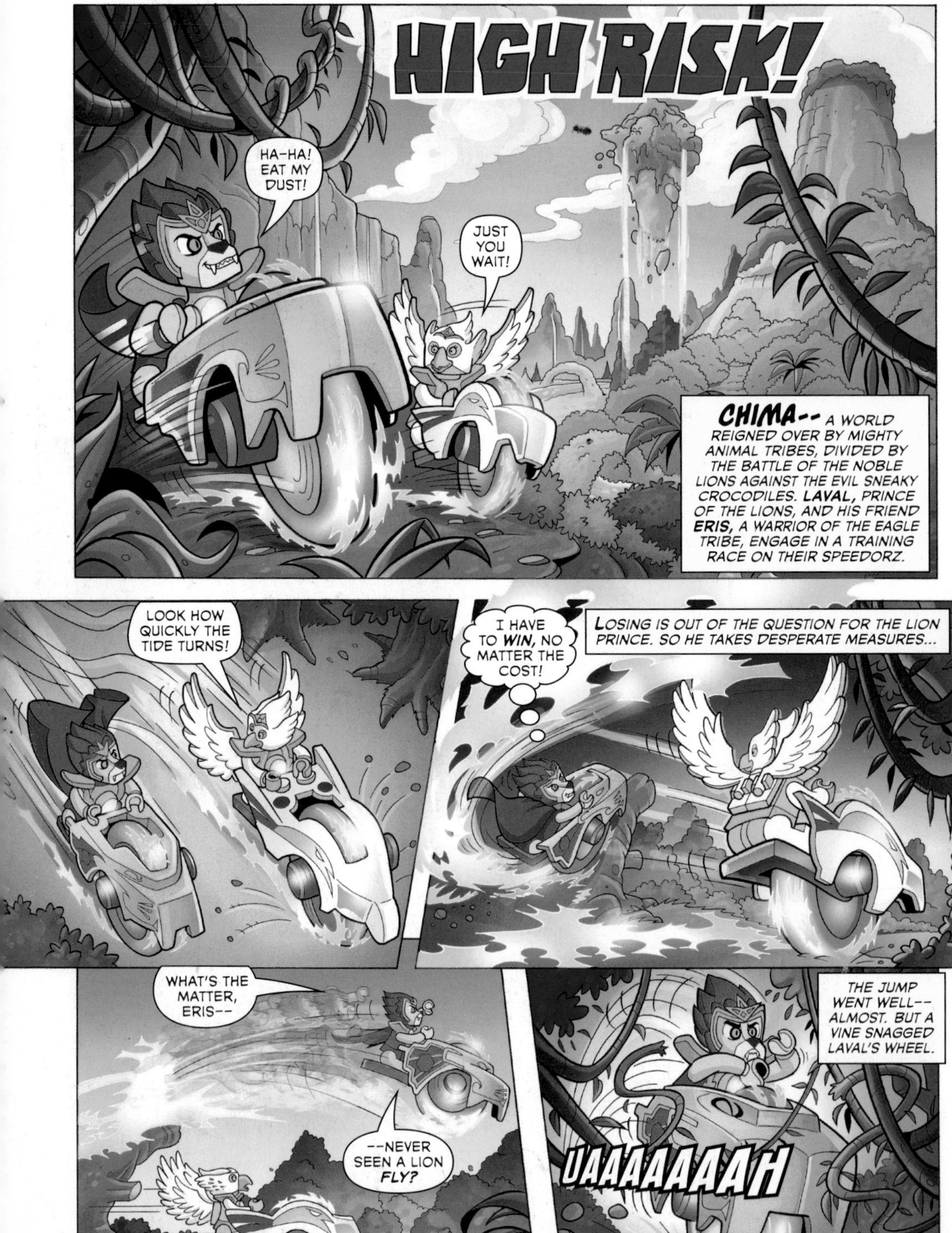
HIGH RISK!
HA-HA! EAT MY DUST!
JUST YOU WAIT!
CHIMA-- A WORLD REIGNED OVER BY MIGHTY ANIMAL TRIBES, DIVIDED BY THE BATTLE OF THE NOBLE LIONS AGAINST THE EVIL SNEAKY CROCODILES. LAVAL, PRINCE OF THE LIONS, AND HIS FRIEND ERIS, A WARRIOR OF THE EAGLE TRIBE, ENGAGE IN A TRAINING RACE ON THEIR SPEEDORZ.
LOOK HOW QUICKLY THE TIDE TURNS!
I HAVE TO WIN, NO MATTER THE COST!
LOSING IS OUT OF THE QUESTION FOR THE LION PRINCE. SO HE TAKES DESPERATE MEASURES...
WHAT'S THE MATTER, ERIS--
--NEVER SEEN A LION FLY?
THE JUMP WENT WELL-- ALMOST. BUT A VINE SNAGGED LAVAL'S WHEEL.
UAAAAAAAH

LAVAL'S RISK FAILS. ERIS WINS THE RACE.

I WON!

I'M SO SORRY, LAVAL. I WAS SO FOCUSED ON WINNING THAT I DIDN'T REALIZE THAT YOU HAD AN ACCIDENT.

ALRIGHT, ALRIGHT. I WANTED IT TOO MUCH. I WAS CARELESS.

YOU DON'T HAVE TO BE SO CONCERNED WITH WINNING. THERE'S NO SHAME IN LOSING. YOU MUSTN'T RISK YOUR LIFE FOR A GAME.

YOU'RE RIGHT. ⇒SIGH⇐ SINCE THE EVENTS WITH *CRAGGER* I'M JUST NOT THE SAME ANYMORE.

"WE WERE BEST FRIENDS. NOT A DAY WENT BY WITH- OUT US PLANNING SOME MISCHIEF...

"WE NEVER SHOULD HAVE SNUCK IN TO THE SACRED POOL OF CHI. IT CHANGED CRAGGER COMPLETELY.

"ALL OF A SUDDEN WE WERE ENEMIES. MY BEST FRIEND WANTS TO CONQUER ALL OF CHIMA. AND I'M THE ONLY ONE WHO CAN STOP HIM."

NOT FAR AWAY, CRAGGER AND HIS GENERALS ARE FORGING A NEW PLAN...

WE NEED MORE CHI IF WE WANT TO DEFEAT THE LIONS.

MY SCOUTS SPOTTED A CONVOY OF THE GORILLAS TRANSPORTING CHI. WE MUST ATTACK IT!

CRAGGER ISN'T SURE OF HIS SISTER'S PLANS.

DO YOU REALLY THINK FIGHTING THE LIONS WILL LEAD TO ANYTHING? IT WON'T BRING OUR PARENTS BACK.

BUT CROOLER HAS VERY SPECIAL MEANS TO CONVINCE HIM. SECRETLY SHE BLOWS MYSTERIOUS POLLEN IN HIS FACE...

OF COURSE! WE HAVE TO DEFEAT THE LIONS ONCE AND FOR ALL AND CHIMA WILL BE OURS.

YOU'RE RIGHT!

OUR GOAL ISN'T REACHED UNTIL WE CONTROL ALL OF THE CHI!

A SHORT TIME LATER, A CONVOY OF GORILLAS IS TRANSPORTING PRECIOUS CHI FROM THE TEMPLE OF THE **LIONS** TO THEIR HOME...

QUICK, QUICK, DUDES. WE HAVE TO GET THE CHI TO OUR BASE BEFORE IT GETS DARK.

AND BEFORE THE CROCODILE DUDES CAN SPOT US!

TOO LATE! **RAZCAL** ATTACKS WITH A CHI-RAIDER!

RRRAHARR! TAKE THIS, APES!

RETREAT! SAVE YOUR-SELVES!

RAZCAL CHASES THE GORILLAS DIRECTLY INTO A TRAP OF THE CROCODILES.

FINISH THEM AND GET THE CHI!

THE GORILLAS ARE LUCKY. LAVAL AND ERIS HAVE SPOTTED RAZCAL'S RAIDER ON THE HORIZON.

WE HAVE TO HELP THEM!

LAVAL! WE CAN'T GO IN THERE ALONE.

THE GORILLAS ARE TRYING TO FEND OFF THE CROCODILES AND THE WOLVES, BUT THEY DON'T STAND A CHANCE. THEY'RE SURROUNDED AND THEIR NUMBERS ARE FEW.

DON'T WORRY! I KNOW WHAT I'M DOING. BUT CALL FOR REINFORCE-MENTS!

I HOPE SOMEONE SEES THE FLARE...

FOOM

AS LAVAL ALMOST REACHES THE BATTLEFIELD...

NO TIME TO LOSE! THE GORILLAS CAN'T HOLD OUT MUCH LONGER.

Is this the end of Laval?! Don't Miss LEGO LEGENDS OF CHIMA #1 "High Risk!"

Index of Terms

Carnivore: an animal that eats meat.

Ceratopsia: the group that includes dinosaurs with frills and horns (such as Triceratops).

Coprolite: fossilized animal droppings.

Cretaceous: era between 145 and 65 million years ago.

Dinosaur: term created by Sir Richard Owen that means "fearfully great lizard." Dinosaurs were reptiles but had their own distinctive characteristics. (For example, they held their legs directly under their bodies.) All dinosaurs were land-based: none flew and none lived in the water.

Fossil: an animal or vegetable solidified in rock.

Hadrosaurs: the group that includes duck-billed dinosaurs (such as Parasaurolophus).

Herbivore: an animal that lives on plants. The term, "vegetarian," is probably more appropriate than "herbivore," as herbs and grass only appeared a little while after dinosaurs became extinct.

Jurassic: era between 200 and 145 million years ago.

Mammal: an animal with mammary glands, whose females nurse their young.

Omnivore: an animal that eats animals as well as plants.

Ornithischian: a dinosaur with hips like a bird.

Orinthopod: the group that includes many herbivorous dinosaurs, such as Iguanodons.

Paleontology: the science that studies extinct species. Its specialists are paleontologists.

Piscivore: an animal that eats fish.

Plesiosaur: a marine reptile that was almost a dinosaur.

Predator: an animal that attacks its prey to eat it.

Pterosaur: a flying reptile that was almost a dinosaur.

Reptiles: vertebrates that primarily crawl. They currently include crocodiles, lizards, snakes, turtles, and used to include dinosaurs, pterosaurs, and plesiosaurs.

Saurischian: a dinosaur with hips like a lizard.

Sauropod: the group that includes long-neck dinosaurs.

Triassic: era in which dinosaurs appeared, between 250 and 200 million years ago.

G L O S S A R Y

Amargasaurus (Page 42)
Meaning: La Amarga lizard (region in Argentina)
Period: Early Cretaceous (130 to 120 million years ago)
Order/ Family: Saurischia/ Dicraeosauridae
Size: 13 feet long   Weight: 22,000 pounds
Diet: Herbivore
Found: Argentina

Archeopteryx (Page 13)
Meaning: Ancient Wing
Period: Late Jurassic (150 to 145 million years ago)
Order/ Family: Saurischia/ Archaeopterygidae
Size: 2 feet long   Weight: 2 pounds
Diet: Carnivore
Found: Germany, Portugal?

Argentinosaurus (Page 9)
Meaning: Argentine lizard
Period: Late Cretaceous (97 to 93 million years ago)
Order/ Family: Saurischia/ Titanosauridae
Size: 115 feet long   Weight: 175,000 pounds
Diet: Herbivore
Found: Argentina

Carcharodontosaurus (Page 29)
Meaning: Shark-tooth lizard
Period: Early and Late Cretaceous (112 to 93 million years ago)
Order/ Family: Saurischia/ Carcharodontosauridae
Size: 46 feet long   Weight: 15,000 pounds
Diet: Carnivore
Found: Algeria, Egypt, Morocco, Niger

Ceratosaurus (Page 39)
Meaning: Horned lizard
Period: Late Jurassic (155 to 150 million years ago)
Order/ Family: Saurischia/ Ceratosauridae
Size: 20 feet long   Weight: 2,000 pounds
Diet: Carnivore
Found: United States, Tanzania?

Coelophysis (Page 23)
Meaning: Hollow Form
Period: Late Triassic (228 to 203 million years ago)
Order/ Family: Saurischia/ Coelophysidae
Size: 8 feet long   Weight: 65 pounds
Diet: Carnivore
Found: United States

Crylophosaurus (Page 14)
Meaning: Cold Crest Lizard
Period: Early Jurassic (189 to 183 million years ago)
Order/ Family: Saurischia/ Diphlosauridae
Size: 20 feet long   Weight: 1,100 pounds
Diet: Carnivore
Found: Antarctica

Dilong (Page 23)
Meaning: Emperor dragon
Period: Early Cretaceous (128 to 125 million years ago)
Order/ Family: Saurischia/ Tyrannosauroidea
Size: 5 feet long   Weight: 55 pounds
Diet: Carnivore
Found: China

Incisivosaurus (Page 43)
Meaning: Incisor lizard
Period: Early Cretaceous (125 million years ago)
Order/ Family: Saurischia/ Oviraptorosauria
Size: 3 feet long?   Weight: 9 pounds?
Diet: Herbivore?
Found: China

Leaellynasaura (Page 27)
Meaning: Leaellyn's Lizard (daughter of the discoverer)
Period: Early Cretaceous (118 to 110 million years ago)
Order/ Family: Ornithischia/ Hypsilophodontidae
Size: 3 feet long   Weight: 22 pounds
Diet: Herbivore
Found: Australia

G L O S S A R Y

Mamenchisaurus (Page 4)
Meaning: Mamenchi Lizard (in China)
Period: Late Jurassic (161 to 156 million years ago)
Order/ Family: Saurischia/ Mamenchisauridae
Size: 80 feet long   Weight: 45,000 pounds
Diet: Herbivore
Found: China

Microraptor (Page 30)
Meaning: Small thief
Period: Early Cretaceous (121 to 110 million years ago)
Order/ Family: Saurischia/ Dromaeosauridae
Size: 3 feet long   Weight: 2 pounds
Diet: Carnivore
Found: China

Muttaburrasaurus (Page 35)
Meaning: Muttaburra Lizard (The site where it was found)
Period: Early Cretaceous (110 million years ago)
Order/ Family: Ornithischia/ Rhabdodontidae
Size: 23 feet long   Weight: 8,800 pounds
Diet: Herbivore
Found: Australia

Oviraptor (Page 6)
Meaning: Egg thief
Period: Late Cretaceous (85 to 70 million years ago)
Order/ Family: Saurischia/ Oviraptoridae
Size: 2.5 feet long   Weight: 65 pounds
Diet: Omnivore?
Found: Mongolia

Protoceratops (Page 40)
Meaning: First Horned Face
Period: Late Cretaceous (85 to 70 million years ago)
Order/ Family: Ornithischia/ Protoceratopsidae
Size: 6.5 feet long   Weight: 450 pounds
Diet: Herbivore
Found: China, Mongolia

Sauropelta (Page 44)
Meaning: Lizard shield
Period: Early Cretaceous (118 to 110 million years ago)
Order/ Family: Ornithischia/ Nodosauridae
Size: 24 feet long   Weight: 6,600 pounds
Diet: Herbivore
Fossils: United States

Shunosaurus (Page 32)
Meaning: Shu Lizard (Chinese province)
Period: Middle Jurassic (167 to 161 million years ago)
Order/ Family: Saurischia/ Cetiosauridae
Size: 30 feet long   Weight: 6,600 pounds
Diet: Herbivore
Found: China

Sinornithosaurus (Page 16)
Meaning: Chinese lizard-bird
Period: Early Cretaceous (125 to 110 million years ago)
Order/ Family: Saurischia/ Dromaeosauridae
Size: 3 feet long   Weight: 9 pounds
Diet: Carnivore
Found: China

Thescelosaurus (Page 37)
Meaning: Marvelous lizard
Period: Late Cretaceous (67 to 65 million years ago)
Order/ Family: Ornithischia/ Thescelosauridae
Size: 13 feet long   Weight: 220 pounds
Diet: Herbivore
Found: North America

Yutyrannus (Page 21)
Meaning: Feathered tyrant
Period: Early Cretaceous (125 million years ago)
Order/ Family: Saurischia/ Tyrannosauroidae
Size: 30 feet long   Weight: 3300 pounds
Diet: Carnivore
Found: China

Diplodocus   **Ankylosaurus**   Par